DEAD TOWN
HOMEWARD BOUND

THE
DEADWATER SERIES
BOOK 8

OTHER LIVING DEAD PRESS BOOKS

DEAD TOWN
HOMEWARD BOUND

ANTHONY GIANGREGORIO

DEAD TOWN/ HOMEWARD BOUND

Table of Contents

FOREWORD

I don't write forewords anymore, but I felt this book needed one, so I can explain to anyone who has already read Dead Town, exactly why it has been repackaged with Homeward Bound.

You see, between editing anthologies and other authors' novels on a regular basis, my own writing has suffered slightly where I simply don't have the time to sit down and write three hundred page books anymore. But I do have time to slip in a novella or a shorter book than normal between projects.

So back when Dead Town was written, I found myself with a novella of my favorite characters and nothing to do with it. Over the past two years, novellas have been more welcome in the world, but when I had Dead Town written and ready to go, I didn't even consider putting it out as a novella-sized book. So I figured I would package it with two original stories I'd written so I could give the reader a decent page count.

I assumed though the reader wouldn't be super happy to see that the Dead Town story was only a hundred pages, they would still be pleased that I had written it at all and would at least read the added short stories, and then possibly want to try out some of my other books if they liked the writing.

See, when *I am Legend* with Will Smith came out in the theaters a few years ago, the novella was re-released in a three hundred page, mass market book. When I bought it, wanting to finally read the story, I found that the story itself was only a hundred pages, and the rest of the book was filled with short stories by Richard Matheson. It didn't bother me at all, as the story was the size the author wanted it to be, and who was I to be upset if it wasn't bigger? If anything, this small novella had taken on a life of its own, being made into countless movies, and I thoroughly enjoyed the extra short stories in the book.

So that was the genesis of why I released Dead Town along with two other stories.

Okay, so now you see my reasoning behind this. Unfortunately, others did not and were very upset that the Dead Town book wasn't larger and accused me of *fooling* them to the point that unsolicited reviews were so cruel it makes a writer wonder why the hell he should even bother writing anymore.

But deep within those angry reviews was a shred of truth. I hadn't seen it that way at the time, but in hindsight it makes sense about the Dead Town story being shorter than the other Deadwater books, and that the page count had been padded with other stories.

See, I didn't realize there were readers out there that *only* liked my Deadwater series and could care less about my other work.

Because I write mostly zombie stories, I figured most people would read those too as well as the Deadwater series (or I can hope, I suppose).

Woulda, coulda, shoulda; so much for trying to figure out what you readers are thinking out there, and when I look back, it was pretty damn presumptuous of me to even try.

Many people told me not to worry about the Dead Town book, that for every one complainer there were a hundred more readers that were pleased.

But I'm a reader as much as a writer, so this little scenario has always bugged me.

So now I've corrected it. The two short stories that were in Dead Town have been taken out and replaced with a new novella called Homeward Bound that takes Henry and his team back to where it all started.

So though no author likes fans that bitch and moan all the time, in this particular situation I have to tell them thanks. If they hadn't bothered to complain, this new story probably never would have been written, as the plot for Dead Army is already fleshed out and nothing in this new story relates.

But despite what I just said, don't get carried away with the complaining thing, there *is* such a thing as *too much*.

AG

WHAT HAS COME BEFORE

Two years ago, a deadly bacterial outbreak escaped a lab to infect the lower atmosphere across America, unleashing an undead plague on the world.

With rain clouds now filled with a killer bacteria, to venture outside in the rain was tantamount to suicide.

To get caught in the rain and exposed to the bacteria would be an instant death. But that wasn't the end. Once dead, the host body would rise again, becoming an undead ghoul, wanting nothing more than to feed on the flesh of the living.

Eventually, the bacteria burned off in the atmosphere but mankind still wasn't safe. The virus then mutated inside the host, and to be bitten by one of the living dead was a death sentence. Sickness followed by a painful death, only to return as one of the undead.

The United States was torn asunder; civilization collapsing like a house of cards in the weeks after the dead began to walk.

But mankind survived, eking out a dreary existence, always keeping one eye open for the attacking dead.

Only two years after the zombie apocalypse, the world has become a very different place from what it once was. Gone are cell phones, the internet, restaurants and shopping malls; now all lost relics of a culture slowly fading into history.

In this new world, the dead walk and a man follows the rules of the gun, where the strong are always right and the weak are usually dead. Major cities are nothing but blackened husks, nothing but giant tombs filled with walking corpses.

Across America, smaller towns have become small municipalities with makeshift walls protecting them from both living and undead attackers. Strangers are not welcome and are either shot on sight or made to move on, that is, if they are not exploited by the rulers of the towns.

Through the destruction of what once was walks a man, crushing death beneath his steel-tipped boots. Before, he was an ordinary man, living a quiet life with a wife and a career, but the rules have changed and so too, has he adapted, becoming a warrior of death who wields a gun with an iron hand, but shows mercy and wisdom when it is needed.

His name is Henry Watson, and with his fellow companions, Mary, Jimmy, Cindy, Sue and Raven by his side, he travels across a blighted landscape, searching for someplace where the undead haven't corrupted everything they touch; where he can lay his head down in safety.

Though life is fleeting, each breath means the possibility of one more day of life, and a better future for all.

DEAD TOWN

I was seventeen when the contaminated rains first came,
spreading their contagion across the land. At the time, no one
understood what was happening, but we all saw the results.

When the rain fell and touched people, they died and came
back to life.

The walking dead.

I know that sounds crazy, but it's the truth. Hell, if you don't
believe me then just go look outside your window.

You won't see the America of old, now it's like something out of
an old Clint Eastwood Spaghetti western.

I lost most of my family from the rains. Luckily, my uncle took
me and my mother in. But if I thought my life couldn't get any
worse, then when the bacteria or whatever it was inside those
damn zombies mutated, I was dead wrong, if you'll pardon the off
color pun.

Something happened a year after the rains fell. While the clouds had burned off the contaminates, the zombies had become infectious themselves.

Now, if you were bit by a ghoul you didn't just die from infection or sepsis, you would die and come back as one of them.

And so the world became a land of the dead where small towns across the country have barricaded themselves in and large cities are death traps, filled with the walking dead. They were named the deadlands, but not many use it, and most just call it no man's land.

Okay, so I guess I got you caught up.

My name is Tyrell Jenkins if I haven't said it yet, my last name doesn't really matter I suppose, but I added it anyway.

But this story isn't about me. No, this story is about a group of four companions who came through my town a few years back.

You see, we had a constable back then who was a real asshole, pardon my French. He ruled with an iron thumb and was more like the Baron or Boss of the town than a peacekeeper. Donaldson was his name.

He had a ruthless gang of cutthroats to watch his back and the entire town was kept firmly under his thumb, no one brave enough to go against him and risk either dying or what the man would do to a challenger's family if said person lost.

And after he had done just that once or twice, people stopped complaining and just accepted his tyranny as a way of life.

And that was how it was since the dead began to walk.

And it would have stayed that way, too, if not for the arrival of the four companions one dark night.

I was on watch that night when they arrived. They had been on the road for more than a month and were all exhausted, hungry and thirsty. There were two women and two men, the men looking like father and son to one another. And the way they bickered, it was very possible.

The women were both pretty. One was blonde, the other brunette. The women had a defiant fire in their eyes that said whoever they had been before the world fell apart was gone and now there was nothing left but confidence and strength.

The younger man was thin and wiry, but not like a beanstalk. Whatever muscle was there was for strength and his eyes were wild and free. Whatever had brought the world to its knees hadn't touched this young man.

And finally there was the leader of their little group. He wasn't a tall man, maybe 5' 8, but he carried himself with a stature that added more than a foot to his height. He was muscular with a hard jaw and steel blue eyes that showed death and mercy at the same time. His hair was the color of ash, grey with some remaining bits of brown interspaced. On his left hip was strapped a sixteen inch panga and a police issue 9mm Glock rested on the right one. Whoever this man had been before the apocalypse was irrelevant, now he was a killer, no questions asked, molded from the life experiences of traveling through a dead world.

The other three companions also carried firearms, whether it was a .38 S&W, an M-16, or a shotgun. Back then I didn't know too much about firearms, but over the years I've talked to enough people who'd seen these people arrive so that I've managed to piece that time together and have now figured out what each of them were carrying.

Oh, did I mention the name of the leader of the four companions?

It was Watson, Henry Watson.

The younger man was Jimmy Cooper and the women were Cindy Jansen and Mary Roberts.

The four had arrived when the moon was high, and when they were confronted by the security guard on the eight foot high, debris-constructed main wall, Watson called up and said they needed a place to stay for the night. And worst of all, the guard needed to make up his mind fast because there were more than a score of zombies on the four companions' asses, just behind them over the next rise.

The guard of course couldn't authorize anything like that, especially after sundown, and so had to call back to the constable. Donaldson wanted to be informed anytime someone arrived at the main gate after dark.

Our town cut through the middle of interstate 40 in Michigan and anyone traveling south had to come upon us. We had worked for months to fortify our town, making a perimeter wall out of anything we could find, such as old cars and jersey barriers.

So far the wall had held just fine, but also the wall had never been truly tested. Most of the time there would be a few straggler zombies here and there, maybe half a dozen at most, but while the guard tried to contact Donaldson on the radio and inform him about the four new arrivals, the first ghoul appeared over the rise.

Slowly, ponderously, like they were moving underwater, the zombies came over the rise on the trail of the companions.

By the time the last one had reached the rise and was on its way down, there were more than fifty of them. A few were carrying tree branches or rocks, others purses or briefcases, and whether they knew what they were doing or just mimicking one of their number, it didn't matter. They were here now and were a danger, both to the four new arrivals and the safety of the town.

"Come on, what the hell are you doing up there!" Henry snapped at the guard on the radio. There were two more men on watch besides me and the head guard, and a bell was being rung at the far end of the wall, alerting the town there was an attack happening.

But the main part of the town was almost a quarter mile from the wall and it would be at least ten minutes before more men arrived, most being stirred from their beds. You see, everyone would have to run to the wall as there were no functioning vehicles inside the town limits with the exception of Donaldson's two squad cars and a few trucks used for heavy work. This was due to the shortage of gasoline.

But I knew at the time that one truck was down with a bad radiator and the other was getting serviced.

So for the moment, there were only the three guards and myself on the wall, and the four companions outside on the road.

"Maybe we should get the hell out of here, Henry," Jimmy said as he raised his shotgun at the approaching horde of undead.

"No chance, Jimmy, there's too many. Sooner or later we'd have to deal with them. Our only chance is to get behind this wall and into this town," Henry said as he looked back up to the top of the eight foot wall of debris.

"Hey, asshole, we need an answer now! Let us the hell in already!" Henry yelled to the guard, who didn't answer.

Mary shifted uncomfortably, her .38 in her right hand while next to her, Cindy was doing the same, the muzzle of her M-16 now aimed at the ghouls. As for me, I was on top of the wall with my .22 rifle. I was young and that's all they would let me use. My eyes kept shifting from the approaching dead to the four people below.

It was Henry who got the others moving, realizing he might have to fight before being allowed into the town, so he began barking orders to his people.

I could see the four companions below in the torch light and I saw them move into a loose skirmish line, Henry taking point while Jimmy and the women fanned out. With the way they had positioned themselves, there was no way one of them could accidentally shoot another of their team. I could see they worked well together, like a well-drilled military unit, and I wished I could just open the gate and let them in. But I knew if I did this without Donaldson's permission, I would find myself in a land of hurt.

"Here they come!" Henry yelled to me and to whoever else was listening on the wall. I glanced to my left to see Herman, the lead guard, still talking on the radio. I heard a few clipped words such as *well-armed*, and *four of them*.

"Wait for it, don't waste your shots!" Henry yelled to his team and the security guards near me also prepared to fire. Even if the four people below hadn't been there, we still needed to protect the town. Our wall wasn't strong enough to survive this kind of an attack and we all knew it. I felt panic fill my insides and I tried to keep it together.

The truth was, this was the first time I'd seen so many undead in one place before. Even when the rains fell, there were never this many that had died and come back at the same time.

But I checked my rifle and prepared to do my part, knowing the small caliber bullets I was using would only be good if I stayed calm and shot the head of each zombie.

Below me, Jimmy raised his shotgun and was about to fire when Henry called out to him.

"Wait another second, Jimmy. Let 'em get close, so damn close you can't miss."

"Shit, Henry, if they get any closer they could pick my nose!" Jimmy yelled back.

"Just do it, dammit, I know what I'm doing!" Henry snapped back.

Neither of the women said a reply, both only having eyes for the dead.

I, too, felt myself growing in awe of this man below me, someone I had never met before, but immediately wanted to follow. Henry Watson had a natural born ability to lead, you could see it by the way he carried himself. He was a man not afraid to make a decision and if the one he made proved wrong, he would deal with it when it happened.

Herman finally got off the radio and he called out to the other guards.

"Donaldson said we can let them in, but not till it's safe enough so that none of those dead bastards can get in. He was adamant about that, too. They don't get in till it's safe, the town comes first."

He then leaned over the wall and repeated his words to Henry who snarled back, but nodded. I could see the man didn't like Herman's answer, but respected it. After all, the town cared nothing for strangers, and had to look after itself.

"Fine," Henry replied. "But once these roamers are down so help me if you don't open that gate."

"I said I would fucker, I don't lie. The boss man just told me himself!" Herman yelled back, insulted for being questioned by an outsider.

"We'll see," Henry remarked and then he had more important things to worry about as time was up and the ghouls were only a few feet away.

"Okay, people, it's show time!" Henry yelled and drew his Glock from his side and began shooting at the approaching ghouls. I watched the man firing and saw that each time he fired; a zombie went down with half its head missing. The man was an excellent shot and I realized there was a reason he and his friends had survived out in the deadlands for so long.

Jimmy was askance of him and he began pumping his shotgun and firing continuously, the barrage of death taking heads off shoulders and tearing off limbs like they were made of paper. The women weren't idle either, each shooting into the undead crowd, knowing only head shots would see them through this night in one piece.

I could feel the adrenalin of the four people below me as they fought for their lives and I joined in, while near me, the other guards began firing down into the moaning crowd. Bodies began to drop like cordwood, the ghouls climbing over them as they struggled to reach Henry and his team. I began firing and I had no idea if any of my shots found a home. It was dark beyond the torch lights on the wall and I couldn't see the targets too well. But below me the companions had no trouble as shot after shot took down a rotting body.

Then Henry yelled to all within hearing. "Fire in the hole!"

I saw the man was holding a military grade fragmentation grenade. Where he had gotten it I knew not, but I knew what it would do to the approaching zombies.

Jimmy and the women fell back to make room and Henry pulled the pin and tossed the grenade about fifteen feet into the undead crowd. The grenade landed and wobbled a foot until a zombie's foot stopped it.

The zombie kicked the grenade another foot and then the timer ran down and the grenade exploded, sending shrapnel in all directions. One zombie who was almost on top of the blast had its lower half sheared off, the top half plopping to the bloody grass. With entrails and organs spilling out of the opening where its legs once were, it began to crawl along, barely fazed that half its body was gone.

I saw this in a flash of light and then Henry shot a round directly into the crawling zombie's forehead. A black hole blossomed on its brow, but the back of the skull dissolved into brains and bone as the body slumped to the grass.

Henry didn't see this and I watched him turn and shoot another three ghouls in the head with such precision it was like he was a robot, a killing machine with no other directive but to shoot each corpse down.

But though the four companions fought valiantly, there were too many zombies and before they knew it they were in a hand to hand brawl as they fought for their lives. I saw Henry holster his Glock when it cycled dry and pull his panga from the sheath on his hip.

With a throaty yell, he sliced at a zombie's neck, taking off the head in one swipe. The head fell to the road to be kicked by shambling feet, a wayward soccer ball with hair.

Hands were sheared off as the panga sung a song of death and destruction, and as I watched, I found myself enthralled by this man, this warrior of the dead.

But I wasn't watching what I was doing as I was too preoccupied with what the companions were doing and I slipped, my left foot sliding off the wall as I felt myself tumble into the air.

Wind rushed past my face and then I felt a jarring impact when my body landed heavily on the road.

I was dead, I was surrounded by zombies and I was saying my prayers as three ghouls came for me, but no sooner did they reach out for me than their hands were lopped off and Henry reached down and grabbed my shirt collar, pulling me up and to safety behind him.

"Come on, kid, no lying down on the job. Use that damn gun!"

He was referring to my .22 which I'd taken with me in my fall and I felt revitalized though in pain, my side hurting from my rough landing. With Henry slicing and dicing near me, I began to shoot again, the bullets from my rifle finding targets. It wasn't hard to do this as there were so many to shoot.

Jimmy was laughing as he blew apart the zombies, his powerful blasts decapitating bodies and blowing arms and legs off. One ghoul got a shot to the face, the head disintegrating into a bloody pink and brown spray. The body, now headless, seemed to dance a jig and then it toppled over to lie still, while its brethren stepped over it. But then the next blast took a walking dead man in the chest, blowing a hole big enough to roll a bowling ball through.

But the dead man never slowed and Jimmy found himself being attacked. Thinking quickly, he jammed the shotgun through the hole in the ghoul so that the muzzle was now poking out the dead man's back, just below the shoulder blades, while the pale face was inches from Jimmy's face.

Jimmy squeezed the trigger, the shotgun belching fire and five more ghouls were taken out as different parts of their anatomy disintegrated in a blood spray. But Jimmy still had the zombie with the hole in its torso to deal with and he found this one had gotten too close to him. He shifted the shotgun and the dead man was moved to the side, but he couldn't get enough room to remove the barrel from the torso.

The teeth of the dead man were snapping near Jimmy's face and it was all he could do to prevent them from taking a piece of his nose off. Deciding he needed a new tactic, Jimmy let go of the shotgun and drew a nine inch Bowie survival knife from a sheath on his belt.

With a yell of anger, he slammed the blade up to the hilt into the dead man's left ear, black ichor seeping around the knife as he twisted it, slicing the brains within to mush. Withdrawing the blade, the ghoul twitched and fell away, the shotgun now sliding out of the hole, Jimmy still having one hand on the weapon.

Then he turned and fired again, the matter of his near death experience irrelevant to the moment.

As for the women, Cindy, her blonde hair flying about her like a halo, sprayed the ghouls on full auto. The bullets of her M-16 ran up the torsos of the zombies until they finally found their heads.

Then, like exploding melons, the heads would erupt in amazing kaleidoscopes of reds and browns as brains splattered the ground and nearby ghouls. One ghoul got a skull fragment in its right eye and it became half-blind. But still it came on, at least until Mary put a bullet in the remaining eye, thus ceasing the advance of the ghoul forever.

Mary was like a wild woman, her beautiful face curled into a rictus of anger. As she killed each zombie, I saw this was something personal to her and I wondered what had happened to make her feel so angry toward these mindless beasts. Later, I would hear about her near death experience on the outskirts of Pittsfield and how she had almost been killed when her own bullet had almost taken her life.

But for now she was a mystery, as were the others.

"Fall back, fall back, there's too damn many!" Henry yelled.

I had to agree. The guards above weren't shooting very many, I saw. Herman was only shooting the zombies that would try to scale the wall. The others he left to Henry and his people. Herman was saving ammunition while risking the companions' lives. And I realized very quickly he was now risking my life, too.

I was now trapped with the strangers outside the wall and I wouldn't be getting back inside unless these zombies were put down.

More than half were down now though, but that left at least another twenty-five or thirty. It was hard to count as the shifting shadows continued to dance across the shapes of the bodies.

To my left, Cindy was spraying a pair of zombies wearing police uniforms and she was amazed when they didn't go down despite multiple shots to the chest. She looked at her rifle like it was broken, or perhaps wondering if she had suddenly begun shooting blanks without realizing it.

Jimmy moved up next to her and pointed at the dead cops.

"They're wearing bullet proof vests, babe, take out their fucking heads!"

Her eyes showed understanding and she shifted her aim higher. Though the headshots wasted ammo, they were more difficult, she zeroed in on her targets. With these two ghouls she had no choice.

The bullets pounded into the desiccated frames until the rounds found the two heads. Skulls exploded in a wide arc, black brains and maggots following along for the ride. The two cops twitched and dropped to the pavement, now without their heads.

"Henry, we can't keep this up! I'm almost out of ammo!" Mary screamed as she shot a dead husband and wife, both falling to the road to be forever entwined in death. Swinging her aim, she took out three men in biker jackets, their logo emblazoned on their backs. But the team they were part of now didn't refer to motorcycles or raising hell, now all they did was eat and kill.

Mary put them down and moved closer to Henry, while Jimmy and Cindy did the same.

I stood behind all four of them, my face as white as a ghost which was a feat as my complexion was normally a dark brown. I was petrified and it was all I could do not to wet myself. As I looked at the side of Henry's face, I was so jealous of this man who stayed in control even in the face of certain death.

"We need to combine our firepower, everyone, line up and on my say take down the ones directly in front of you!"

The companions did as they were ordered, each making a firing line.

"You," Henry told me. "Get next to me and just do what I say if you want to live past the next minute."

I obeyed on instinct, knowing this man was my only hope to survive this night, and as I waited for his next barked order, Henry took three steps forward of the others, like he was now the top of a triangle.

He popped out his clip and slapped in a fresh one, wanting to know he had at least seventeen rounds ready to go, and then he raised his left hand which still held the panga.

"Okay, ready! Take the bastards out!"

No sooner did he lower the panga then he and the other three companions began firing. But where before the shooting had been wild, now it was controlled, each focusing on a particular area in the attacking zombie horde. Bodies were blown off their feet as each warrior took down the dead and I began firing as well, knowing it was our only hope for salvation.

Above, on the wall, Herman stopped firing into the undead horde; enjoying the show the five of us were giving him and his men. I did see Henry glance up once to see Herman wasn't defending the wall and I saw Henry scowl deeply.

For the next two minutes, the area in front of the main gate was filled with gunfire and cordite, smoke wafting high into the night sky as brass shells fell to the ground like confetti at a parade, littering the road and causing the footing to become treacherous.

And then, just as suddenly as it began, it was over, the last gunshot reverberating across the road to fade away into the night sky.

No one spoke for more than fifteen seconds, each person breathing heavily as they wiped sweaty brows and took stock of themselves.

Then Henry broke the silence as he gazed up at Herman who was grinning widely at the show.

"Okay, they're all down, now open that goddamn gate or so help me you'll be joining these roamers in Hell!"

Herman didn't move at first, he just stared down at the five of us, as if he was weighing his options. Then he nodded and with a gesture to one of the other guards, he said. "You heard the man, open the damn gate; they got 'em all. They earned passage into our town."

There was another minute of silence and I was beginning to wonder if Herman was going to double cross these four people. I'd seen it done before, but I was surprised if he would try it now. After the way these four people had taken down ten times their number was a feat not seen often and I would expect Herman to understand that these were formidable warriors.

And then the gate began to open, the rusting hinges creaking loudly, as another guard stepped out of the open gate and onto the road. I could see he was uncomfortable, now out in the field and not behind the protective wall, and I wanted to laugh and ask him to come stand where I'd been for the past few minutes.

The guard waved Henry and the others inside, and with a glance to his friends who nodded they were with him, Henry turned and strode through the gate, the rest of his team right behind him.

"Well, Tyrell, you comin' or what?" The guard asked me.

Shaken from my stupor I nodded. "Hell, yeah, I am," I said and then ran through the gate, the guard closing it with a loud click.

My shift was almost done anyway. The next morning a work detail would come out to the wall and take care of the bullet riddled corpses, carrying or dragging them a ways down the road where they would burn the lot of 'em.

As for me, I was excited about the four new guests to my town. I already owed Henry a debt for saving my life, but there was another reason, too.

Seeing how Henry Watson carried himself and the way he acted, I just knew when he met Donaldson there would be sparks a flyin'. The thing was, at the time, I just didn't realize just how big those sparks were gonna be.

With the excitement for the night over, Herman left the security of the wall to one of his men and led Henry and company into town.

After what had happened to me, no one seemed to care about what I was doing, so I decided to follow the companions into town to see what was going on. With a wave to the remaining guards on the wall, I followed at a discreet distance, barely hearing the words spoken by Herman to Henry.

But from what I could hear, Herman was filling in the companions on how things were run in our town and how they better step lightly or pay the price.

Henry replied that they didn't want any trouble and just wanted to rest for a day or two. Jimmy commented on how were they going to get reimbursed for all the ammunition expended in the battle, but all Herman did was laugh as he picked up his pace.

Eventually, Herman slowed and then stopped in front of what was once the local movie theater for our fair town. But movies were a thing of the past and the entire building had been gutted and was now both saloon and meeting house for the town.

There were a few men standing at the large, double doors, smoking, with mugs of homebrewed beer in their hands and they stepped aside at the sight of Herman approaching.

Herman barely noticed them, used to people getting out of his way. The whole town knew Herman had Donaldson's ear so no one messed with him if they didn't have to.

The companions followed Herman inside and then just as I was about to go in too, I felt a hand come down heavily on my shoulder.

"And where do ya think you're goin', Tyrell?"

My heart dropped in my chest at the sound of that voice. I knew it instantly. It was Bubba, the bouncer for the saloon. He was well over six feet and had so much hair on his chest, back and arms that he looked like a gorilla.

Swallowing the knot in my throat, I gestured to the retreating backs of Mary and Cindy.

"I'm going in there, with them. I want to see what's gonna happen next?"

Bubba shook his head. "Nothin' doin', squirt, the world may be in the shitter, but Donaldson said you still gotta be over eighteen to get into this bar. He says it ain't a daycare in there, it's a place for men ta drink." He leaned over and grinned widely. "Ya feel me?"

I cringed as he said that, as if because I was black he thought he could talk in slang. But I knew better then to say anything.

"Yeah, Bubba, I feel you. I'll go."

"Good," Bubba said and then slapped me on the shoulder so hard I almost went to my knees. Wincing, I walked out of the large hallway as I rubbed my shoulder. That friendly tap was to get his point across and normally it would have. I'd tried to sneak into the bar before but was always caught.

But this time was different. Henry and his friends were in there and I couldn't tell you why, but I knew I wanted to know what was going to happen next in there.

Donaldson was in the bar as that was where he always was if he wasn't out harassing the townspeople. I just had to see how that meeting between Henry and him went.

As I stepped outside, I cast a glance back to the theater and I knew I had to find a way inside, and as I began to wander away, my mind working on a solution to my problem, I found one just as quick.

It was as I was passing the side alley to the right of the theater that I heard a ruckus, like trashcans being rattled. Jogging over and peering into the alley, I saw one of the workers of the bar tossing a couple of bags of trash out.

As I watched, the worker went back in, the door slowly closing, as if it was in slow motion. Seeing my chance, I darted for the door and managed to reach it just before it clicked shut.

Ah-ha, I had my in, and as I slipped inside into the cool gloom of the back of the movie theatre which would bring me to the saloon, my heart began to beat with the excitement of what might come next.

* * *

The second I entered the section that was the saloon, I could smell the odor of men who didn't bathe and the redolence of cheap homebrew and rolled cigarettes.

I knew the real alcohol had run out more than six months ago, but I also knew the homebrew stuff could either clean the paint off the side of a car or knock you flat on your ass in less than a minute.

As I crept through the storeroom filled with empty bottles and other miscellaneous items, I reached a dirty curtain that was used instead of a door.

Peeking through the side of the material, I saw the saloon in all its degenerate splendor. There were about twenty men and women scattered at the odd assortment of tables and chairs. The furniture had been salvaged from a diner, offices, and a few homes, now all of it scattered about the floor like a drunk decorator had gotten a free hand at the place.

To the right was the bar, the long counter spread almost fifteen feet from wall to wall. It was made of plywood and pressure-treated wood and only the dark stain made it look even halfway like a respectable counter.

Off to the left was a small stage. This was where the old nylon sheet had once been for movies, but now it was torn down, the stage used for assemblies and sometimes live music.

In the middle of the main floor was where I could see Donaldson. He was sitting at the head of a large dining room table and on each side of him, six men deep, were his cronies. These men always had his back and were the reason Donaldson was still the constable of our town.

As I watched, my eyes taking in the scantily clad women moving from table to table, and the waitresses who were wearing about the same, I spotted Herman coming in from the front of the saloon. Behind him were the four companions, each now trying to look in every direction at once.

Henry was still in the lead, right behind Herman, and I saw his hand slowly go down to rest on his Glock, as if just knowing it was there made him feel better about where he was.

Luckily I was close enough to hear everything that was said once Herman reached Donaldson.

"Hey, Boss, these are the four I was tellin' you about," Herman said as he stopped in front of Donaldson. He quickly introduced each of the companions to him and then did the same for the four outsiders, though he'd already filled them in on the walk over from the gate.

The constable was a big man, well over six feet and his broad shoulders said he had done some weight lifting in his past. But the muscle was still hard and the jaw was still strong. Donaldson leaned forward in his chair and placed his ham-sized fists on the table.

On his hip he wore a pair of Colt .357 Magnums and the badge on his chest was a slap in the face for each townsperson when they saw it. What that badge represented was now a joke of past rules and honor. Now all that badge represented was oppression.

"So these are the heroes," Donaldson said over the music from the juke box in the corner. There was the sound of a generator purring behind one of the walls; this was the reason there was power for the overhead lights, the music, and a few other necessities such as the blender behind the bar. You can't make a mixed drink without a blender and the power kept the ice machine running, one of the few luxuries left to our small town.

"Well, I wouldn't say that," Henry replied as he sized up the man in front of him. His eyes played across the other men at the dining room table besides Donaldson and he saw hard men, what he called coldhearts. These were men who would cut out your heart and feed it to you while it beat its last.

"You wouldn't?" Donaldson asked as he sized up Henry and then let his eyes roam over Jimmy and the women. He let his eyes linger on Mary and Cindy, but then they flicked back to Henry. "Seems to me you saved our town single-handedly, well, that is the four of you did. That's some serious firepower you're packin' there. I hope we won't have any trouble with you 'cause we let you keep 'em."

Henry moved his head back and forth very solely. "Not as far as I can see. We just want to rest up and get some food, then in a day or so we'll head on out. Figure we earned it, don't you think?"

"Fuck yeah, we earned it, used up all our damn ammo, too," Jimmy added under his breath.

Donaldson attention shifted from Henry to Jimmy. "You got somethin' to say, boy?"

"Huh, oh, yeah, it's just; we used all our ammo saving your town and now what have we got to show for it? Way I see it, you owe us big-time."

"Jimmy, shut the hell up," Henry hissed.

"No, Watson, that's all right, let the man speak. After all, he did save us from the bad ol' zombies tryin' to eat us." As he said this he sounded like a scared little boy and his cronies all chuckled. Henry knew the man was baiting him, but he kept it reined in, knowing this was the leader of the town, but Jimmy, in his head-strong ways wasn't getting it.

"Hell, yeah, we saved you from all those roamers," Jimmy added. "If it wasn't for us, you'd have your asses gettin' bitten off as we speak."

Henry glanced to Cindy and Mary who only shrugged. Neither wanted to say anything just yet, not knowing where it was going. Both had hands near their weapons and had flicked safeties off just to be on the safe side.

Henry watched Donaldson's face go hard and he was tensing for trouble when suddenly, the constable's face lightened and he began to laugh.

"You know what, boy? You're right, you did, and me and this town owe you a debt of thanks. Tell you what, the first rounds on me, in gratitude."

"What? Are you fucking serious? A round of drinks for almost getting our asses eaten? That's bullshit!" Jimmy snapped.

Henry watched Donaldson face grow dark and he realized the man was only egging Jimmy on. Stepping in, Henry placed a hand on Jimmy's shoulder, silencing him.

"That sounds real nice, Donaldson. A drink would wash the dust out of my mouth, thanks for that." He then quickly turned to face Jimmy, so that Donaldson couldn't see him. "Come on, Jimmy, let's get that drink." He mouthed the word now as he squeezed Jimmy's bicep.

"But, Henry, the guy just..."

"Now, Jimmy, I'm thirsty." Henry glared at Jimmy, hoping the younger man wouldn't be as obtuse as he usually was. There were times when Jimmy's one track mind was a danger to them all.

Finally Jimmy got it, though he wasn't happy about it.

"Fine, a drink would be nice." Jimmy turned to look at Donaldson. "That's nice of you, thanks," he growled through gritted teeth.

Donaldson had a wide grin on, knowing he was messing with Jimmy, insulting him by only offering a round of drinks for all that the companions had done.

"Anytime, boy, now go on over to the counter, Marvin will set you up with whatever you want."

Jimmy locked his eyes with Donaldson and held them for a full twenty seconds, but eventually he lowered his gaze, doing it for Henry and the women.

Then he moved away with Mary and Cindy, who had remained silent the entire time. A few of Donaldson's men watched the two women move away, admiring the shape of their hips and buttocks. Both women filled out a pair of jeans like fashion models and many a head turned as they passed. With the guns on their hips or across their shoulders, it was an odd contrast to their natural beauty.

"Got yourself a real hothead there, don't ya, Watson," Donaldson commented as he leaned back in his chair and folded his arms across his wide chest.

"Perhaps, but can't blame him, can you? We used a lot of ammo up and all you give us is a round of drinks?"

Donaldson's slightly smiling face suddenly went hard and then the man leaned forward again.

"I let you into my town, didn't I? Way I see it that's reward enough." He pierced Henry with his gaze as he signaled the men near him to stand up, now all six slightly surrounding Henry. "Don't you think that's reward enough?"

Henry looked at each man now glaring at him and knew this was a fight he couldn't win. He was outgunned.

"Yeah, I guess it is, and I just wanted to thank you once more for doing that. Me and my friends are grateful."

Donaldson stared at Henry for almost a full minute, sizing him up some more, but when Henry's face didn't flinch after his comment, eventually Donaldson signaled his men to sit down again.

"That's fine Watson, just as long as you know what's what around here and you know your place. I'm the law and fuck with me and you'll end up in a ditch at the back of the town. You got one day here. Rest up and eat then get going. We use the barter system around here. Bullets and guns work the best, but there are other ways too, such as using your women in trade for a few rolls in the sack with some of my men. That'll get you as much jack as you'll need, I'll see to that."

One of Donaldson's men spoke up then. "Hey, Boss, I'd pay good jack for a try at the blonde."

Donaldson nodded to his man then looked back to Henry. "You heard Bob, Watson, how 'bout it? Let him take the blonde for a spin and it'll get you enough jack for your stay here."

"No, I don't think so, they're not whores, they're my friends. We'll pay with bullets if it's all the same to you."

Donaldson leaned back again, as if the matter was closed.

"Fair enough, but ya can't blame Bob for asking, after all, the blonde is a nice piece of ass."

Henry said nothing, only stared at Donaldson. His hands were tight as he fought to control himself. He could see this man was an asshole, like so many he'd met along his travels since the world fell apart, and he wanted to pull his Glock and put a bullet in the constable's head, right between the eyes. But he knew what would happen if he tried so he held off. Just rest up for a day and then leave, that would be the plan and he wanted to stick with it.

"Can I go join my people? I'm thirsty," Henry said in a flat voice.

"Sure, go, we're done here. But you should know, I'll be watching you."

Henry nodded, turned and moved away with a, "Wouldn't be the first time I was watched."

Then he was at the counter with the others.

I watched all of this with baited breath from behind the curtain. I'd thought a few times there was gonna be trouble, but was relieved when nothing happened, the heavy sigh leaving my mouth lost in the rumble of the saloon. But it still wasn't over. I could see Donaldson's men now casting furtive glances to the companions as the rest of the people in the saloon went about their revelry as if it was any other day. And as I watched, I saw Bob keep casting lecherous glances to Cindy, who didn't notice she was under scrutiny.

And it was when Bob leaned forward and began talking silently with Donaldson that I knew something was up, so I got more comfortable and watched, wondering if the four companions were going to make it out of the saloon alive after all.

Henry ordered a round of the homebrewed beer for himself and his friends and drank greedily when it arrived.

"What're you gonna pay me with? Only the first round is free," the grizzled bartender inquired, his throat sounding like a pile of dried leaves blown in the wind, thanks to too much smoking.

Henry reached into his pocket and pulled out a few rounds for his Glock. The 9mm bullets rolled a little until coming up against the bartender's hand.

"Here, that should take care of us for the night," Henry told him.

The bartender scooped up the bullets like they were loose change and shook his head. "That won't cover much," he said

Henry leaned over the counter so he was looking straight into the bartender's eyes.

"Do I look like I was born yesterday, asshole? I just pissed away three clips saving this godforsaken town, and your ass, too. I think that's gonna be just enough, don't you?" His eyes creased to mere slits and his jaw went taut.

The bartender held Henry's gaze for less than five seconds and then looked away, deciding it wasn't worth it.

"Yeah, I guess so. After all, you did help out the town. Okay, two more rounds and then you're done."

Henry knew he was still being screwed, but in the end it didn't matter. None of the group would be drinking more than three beers anyway. If they got drunk and sloppy they might end up dead. Oh, no, this wasn't the place to relax and kick up their heels.

A man with a long beard and the stench of cooking oil wandered over to Mary.

"Hey, there, sweet thing, how 'bout you come over to my table for a bit. I'll buy you a drink and everythin'."

"No thank you, I'm with my friends, perhaps another time," Mary replied politely, hoping that would be enough to deter the man.

But her hopes were dashed when he turned to his buddies and they coaxed him to continue.

"Ah, come on, sweet thing, we'll take good care of you."

Henry noticed Mary was having a problem and he turned to her.

"You need some help?"

She shook her head, her brown tresses caressing her cheeks and shoulders.

"No, Henry, I got it," she grinned at first, but then her visage went hard and she turned to the man. Deciding he wouldn't take no for an answer, Mary moved in and grabbed the man by his balls, gripping the testacles through the seat of his pants. The man let out a soft yelp, startled by her reaction to his advances.

"Now look, mister, I appreciate your invitation and everything, but as you can see, I'm with my friends. Now you can do one of two things. You can take my answer and leave or I can make sure you're never able to father a child again." She squeezed harder, causing the man to wince. "So, what's it going to be?"

"I'll leave," he gasped, "sorry to have bothered you."

"Good choice," Mary replied and let him go.

As he stumbled away, a few men standing nearby who had witnessed the event were laughing, causing the man more humiliation.

Jimmy chuckled as he took a pull of his beer.

"Damn, Mary, remind me not to get you mad at me. I wouldn't want you doing that to me."

She wiped her hand clean on a dirty napkin and shrugged, smiling slightly.

"I wouldn't do it to you anyway, Jimmy, I wouldn't be able to get my hand around something that small."

"Hey," Jimmy exclaimed. "That hurt." He turned to Cindy. "Aren't you gonna stick up for me, babe?"

Cindy only shrugged as she watched the saloon and the faces around her, searching for any possible signs of danger. "Can't, you forget, I've seen it for myself."

Jimmy looked dejected, but he knew when to shut up, so turning back to the counter, he drank his beer silently, using the mirror set up at the rear of the bar, behind the bartender, to keep an eye on the area behind him.

For the next ten minutes, the four companions drank and talked amongst themselves, each keeping a close watch on their surroundings. Henry was just about to suggest they leave when another man came up to the women, this one heading directly towards Cindy.

It was Bob, Donaldson's man, and he moved up to Cindy and slapped her ass like he owned her.

"Hey, sweetheart, why don't you let me by ya a drink," he said with a lecherous grin. His eyes were staring at her chest as he spoke, like two cameras locked on their targets.

"Hey, what the hell? You big oaf, try that again and I'll stick my gun up your ass and squeeze the trigger," Cindy snapped back as she spun after feeling the slap to her ass.

Jimmy spun at the same time and stepped up to Bob.

"Hey, asshole, that's my girlfriend you just slapped."

Bob laughed as he looked down on Jimmy. With the two men standing eye to eye, Jimmy had to look almost straight up. Bob had more than a hundred pounds on him and shoulders nearly twice as wide. If Bob and Jimmy mixed it up, it could be a massacre... for Jimmy

Jimmy had a memory of a similar situation that had happened when he first met Cindy. But then he'd gotten lucky; he didn't know if he would do so again if he tried to take this behemoth of a man out.

Henry had seen what was happening and was watching things closely. He knew Jimmy was his own man and would let him handle his own fights, though, he too, wanted to jump in. But he knew if he did, then Jimmy would never forgive him for it, so he bit his tongue and watched the rest of the saloon for trouble.

"Henry, do something," Mary hissed askance of him.

"He's a big boy, Mary, he has to fight his own battles, still, keep an eye out for more trouble.

"Okay," she replied as she watched Jimmy stand up to the man twice his size. She had to admit her friend had courage. Cindy was there, too, trying to get the two men to separate.

"Step aside, little man, and I won't step on you like a bug," Bob warned as he shoved Jimmy away from him. Jimmy was only a foot from the counter, so when he was pushed back, his shoulders struck the counter, stopping him. No sooner did he hit the counter then he was off, lunging at Bob like a missile shot out of its tube.

Bob, being so large, was used to his size intimidating everyone in the town into submission. He wasn't used to anyone, let alone someone the size of Jimmy, to actually be crazy enough to even think of attacking him. Before he knew what was happening, Jimmy was on him, the smaller man's elbow cracking his chin and Jimmy's knee went up into his crotch.

Any other man and the two blows, simultaneously delivered, would have laid that man out, but Bob barely felt it. Other than a soft *whoosh*, out of his mouth, he remained standing.

Jimmy stood perfectly still, as did Cindy next to him, both not knowing what to do. Bob began to laugh, while behind him, more men approached, each also laughing.

Bob continued to laugh until he felt something cold press against the side of his neck and he glanced down to see Henry's hard visage and the muzzle of the Glock jammed into the soft folds of his neck.

Bob stopped laughing then, understanding if Henry squeezed the trigger, he'd be dead, his brains splattering across the closest table.

"I think this little argument is over," Henry hissed, and as he spoke the words the music stopped like a record needle had been slid and then taken from the surface, and every face in the room turned to the counter.

There was a muffled hush and then the men standing behind Bob each pulled their weapons, an odd assortment of firearms from derringers to snub-nosed specials to an old WW2 antique that looked like it would blow up in the owners hand if he was foolish enough to try and fire it.

No sooner did the men pull their guns then Cindy, Jimmy and Mary each drew theirs, all muzzles now facing the opposite team.

Henry never flinched as guns were cocked and hammers pulled back, prepared to shoot him full of a dozen rounds of lead.

The bouncer Bubba came running in and when he saw all the guns, he quietly turned and went back outside. He was just muscle, firearms weren't his thing. He knew Donaldson was in the bar and he would let his boss handle things.

Then the men aiming guns at the companions parted and Donaldson strolled between them, stopping three feet from Henry. He could see the Glock jammed into Bob's throat and could see the tension Henry's finger had on the trigger. He knew if one of his men fired, Henry would take Bob with him into that dark night.

"Shit, Watson, you haven't been here for an hour and you're already starting trouble. What the fuck am I gonna do with you? Bob just wanted to buy the lady a drink."

Henry shrugged casually, like the two of them were chatting about the weather.

"Don't ask me, Donaldson, ask your man here. It seems he doesn't know how to take no for an answer, and worse thing is he has grabby hands." Henry pushed the Glock in a half inch deeper and Bob winced in pain. "Didn't your momma ever teach you to treat a lady with respect?"

A sheen of sweat was on Bob's forehead now.

"I asked you a question, big guy," Henry hissed.

"Y...y...y...yes, sir, she did," Bob stuttered.

"Really, then why would you go and do the shit you just did?"

"Listen, Watson, you let him go right now or you and your people are dead," Donaldson warned.

"That's not the way I see it, Donaldson. You shoot and we won't go down alone." Henry glanced to Jimmy. "Hey, Jimmy, who you gonna take out first?"

"Him, of course," Jimmy said as he stared at Donaldson.

"Hmmm," Henry mused. "Seems we got ourselves one of them Mexican standoffs, well, that is unless you want to get blood all over this nice floor under our feet." His eyes flicked to Donaldson, to Bob, and back to Donaldson. "So, what's it gonna be, Boss? We can wrack this up to a misunderstanding or it can get bloody. It's up to you. Me? I'm ready to die." Henry shoved the muzzle in deeper still as he moved closer to Bob. "How 'bout you, Bob? You ready to die today?"

No one moved, each man and the two women all holding their guns on one another, fingers on triggers. All it would take was less than a half ounce of pressure, or one cough, and all Hell was about to break loose in the deathly quiet saloon.

Henry gritted his teeth as he pressed the Glock deeper still into Bob's neck.

"Well, Donaldson, what's it gonna be?"

Bob gulped deeply, then closed his eyes and swallowed as he waited for the bullet to blow his brains across the room.

I watched the deadly standoff play out from behind the curtain with my mouth hanging open. I'd never seen someone stand up to Donaldson like this and I knew any second there was going to be a gunfight in the saloon like there never had been before.

And I knew all four of the companions would most likely be killed.

I couldn't let that happen, not after Henry had saved my life.

So I did something I never would have believed possible. As the standoff continued, I charged into the saloon from behind the curtain, knocking a waitress into a table as I dashed towards the men.

When I reached them, I went in between every gun in the room. I swallowed the knot of fear in my throat as I saw all those gun barrels now aimed at me. They sure looked bigger than their one inch circumference when you know each one would spell death in an instant.

"What the fuck?" Donaldson, spit. "Tyrell, get your black ass out of here before I have you shot!"

"No, wait, Mr. Donaldson, please, you don't understand who these people are!"

"What the hell are you talkin' about?" Donaldson asked, his face filled with anger.

And that's when I filled him in on exactly what happened at the main gate and how Henry had saved me and how the rest of the companions had fought so valiantly. I didn't say anything about Herman, though I wanted to.

I knew if I told Donaldson how Herman had held his fire and risked the town, the constable would have been pissed and later, after Herman had been chastised, it would be my turn.

When I was finished, Donaldson's visage took on a different aspect. There was slightly more respect there for Henry and the rest of his group than before.

I stood perfectly still, not wanting to move and risk an itchy trigger finger sending me to Hell and then, with a chuckle, Donaldson raised his hands for his men to lower their weapons.

"Goddamn, Tyrell, if that's what went down then damn, I have to give Watson here another thank you." He stepped towards Henry, his face now less threatening, and he patted Bob on the shoulder as if he was telling him things would be fine. Bob didn't agree as the Glock was still jammed into his neck.

"Watson, if even half of what Tyrell just said is true than you did a helluva thing out there today. Tell ya what, let Bob here go and we'll pretend this shit never happened. Fair enough?"

Henry studied Donaldson's visage, trying to see if the man was telling the truth.

"And what if I told you to go to Hell?" Henry asked casually.

"Well, then I guess we could go back to pointing guns at one another and then when it all goes to shit we can shoot each other down. Me, I think I'd rather just let it all go. So what do ya say? I'm only gonna ask you once, Watson, take it or leave it."

Henry glanced to Jimmy and the women, the latter two each nodding, though Jimmy shrugged. He was always itching for a fight, but even he saw the hopelessness of the standoff.

"Whatever you want to do, old man, its fine with me," Jimmy said.

Henry seemed to weigh his prospects. Grunting an okay, he removed the Glock from Bob's throat. As he did, there was now a bright-red impression from the muzzle and the sight on the end had drawn a small pinprick of blood. Bob stepped back and rubbed his neck.

"Asshole, this shit ain't over," he growled.

"Anytime, big man," Henry snarled as he held his Glock at waist level. All it would take was a casual flick and it would be up again.

"No, Bob, I said this shit is over and it's fucking over, you here me?" Donaldson growled.

"Yeah, Boss, I hear ya," Bob said.

"Good, now get the hell out of here. You've caused enough trouble tonight."

Bob turned and pushed his way through a few of Donaldson's men, leaving the saloon in a huff.

Donaldson turned back to Henry. "So, we good?"

"For now," Henry replied.

Donaldson smiled then, and the gesture wasn't for Henry. He turned and faced his men, all with guns still lowered.

"Okay, you assholes, the fun's over, get back to drinking and whorin'." He turned to one of the waitresses. "Hey, Tammy, get the music back on, this is a bar, not a damn morgue."

The waitress nodded and dashed across the saloon, getting the juke box to play again.

The tension in the air was washed away like a cool breeze over a clear glade and every face in the saloon relaxed.

In less than thirty seconds, the saloon was filled with music, talking and laughter. It was like the altercation had never happened.

Donaldson turned and walked back to Henry.

"I think you should leave in the morning, Watson. I don't need your kind of shit around here. I'm giving you a pass for what you did to Bob because of the help you gave my guards earlier, but the next time I'll have your ass in a sling…and your neck, too. You got me?"

"Yeah, I got you," Henry said. He turned away from Donaldson then, as if he was dismissing him. Donaldson's jaw dropped open, not used to being treated like that, but before he could say anything, Henry was four feet away and next to Jimmy.

"Come on, I think we've had enough excitement for one day, don't you?"

Jimmy nodded. "And then some."

Jimmy reached out and grabbed Cindy's arm, and she went with him as Mary joined Henry.

The four companions headed for the front door to leave the saloon, but Henry paused when he saw me standing to the side, not knowing what to do with myself. I knew sooner or later I was going to be seen and kicked out, but for now I just stood quietly.

Henry waved me over to him.

"Thanks, son, I owe you for what you just did," Henry told me. "I have a feeling that wouldn't have ended too well for anyone."

"No problem, I owed you for saving me at the gate," I said. "If not for you, I'd be in a dead guy's stomach right now or worse, walking around dead until one of the guards took my head off."

Henry nodded at my words. "Well, son, we're even now, that's for damn sure."

He slapped me on the back and then headed out of the saloon. Jimmy flashed me a smile and a wave and the two women also smiled at me.

The blonde was so pretty I had to admit I felt my stomach flutter. Then they were gone and I was all alone.

Donaldson was talking to his men and a few of his cronies were asking why Watson and his people were still alive and Donaldson was explaining to them that with the weapons Henry and his people carried, it would have been some serious casualties on both sides.

So he had made a judgment call and had let the four strangers walk. He now regretted not telling Herman he should've taken their weapons upon them entering the town, but it was too late now.

One of his men told him he was getting soft and Donaldson replied by drawing one of his Magnums and shooting the man point blank in the chest from two feet away.

The man flew backwards, his back becoming a gaping wound as he twitched on the floor in death spasms. Donaldson turned to the rest of his men and asked them if anyone else thought he was getting soft. Of course, no one answered.

No one in the bar paid it any attention and the juke box never stopped playing. If Donaldson wanted to kill his own men, that was fine with everyone else.

I watched for another minute as the dead man was taken out back and then I decided all the action was over for the night and I should get out before I was thrown out, too.

So I left the saloon. As I walked back to my house, where my mother was waiting on me, I would have figured that would be it for the action in our small town for one day.

After all, there had been a large zombie attack and then almost a gunfight in the saloon. That was a lot of excitement for our little town.

But what I didn't know at the time was what had come before was nothing compared to what was coming that night.

I found out about the stuff I wasn't there to see and hear for myself from the townspeople that had witnessed it first hand.

It seemed when Henry and his friends left the saloon, they found out where they could stay for the night from one of Donaldson's men and they headed off down the street.

Two blocks away from the saloon was a small, one-story hotel. It only had ten rooms to let, but even before the rains came that was enough to accommodate the few people who passed through our town.

Mostly the people who stayed overnight with us were salesmen passing though or a few truckers looking to take the scenic route. We weren't anywhere near the main interstates that would get you from A to B fast so we were relatively left alone.

There was a blender factory about ten miles out of town and most of the able bodied men and women had worked there. Ever used a blender? Well, if it was made in the US of A it probably came from our factory, or so we liked to call it. There was also a small mill nearby as well and the two kept the town running just fine.

Of course, now they're all gone, closed for the foreseeable future.

Upon reaching the hotel, the group grabbed a room. But they only took one room, which the hotel manager found odd. He told Henry he had enough rooms for everyone, but Henry was adamant they were fine with the one, though he did ask for a few extra blankets and towels.

See, we had running water in most of the main part of town. A jury rigged, gravity fed supply was set up which led from the higher ground to the west. So far it's worked okay. To a lot of the people in town, life is mostly the same as it ever was. They work and play, all behind the ramshackle walls built to protect them.

If a person doesn't want to face the reality of what's on the other side of our wall, namely the walking dead, then they can most of the time, that is if they aren't involved with the guarding of the town or cleanup of bodies when the dead show up and have to be put down like rabid dogs.

The companions sent out for some food and began to relax after a long day. Henry began stripping their weapons and each of them took turns showering in the small bathroom. Though the water was cold, it still felt like paradise to each of them.

Two hours later, now clean and fed, the latter being peanut butter sandwiches and some fresh tomatoes grown in one of the fields we raise crops in, the four weary travelers bedded down for the night.

It had been a long day and night, and all four of them agreed they were exhausted and wanted to get as much rest as possible. They planned on leaving as soon as the sun was up tomorrow so there was no need to stay awake any longer than necessary.

A pair of Coleman lanterns illuminated the room as each got ready for bed, the women taking the full-size bed, Jimmy the floor, and Henry a chair in the corner. With the town revelers finally heading off to bed outside the hotel, the lanterns were dimmed and the room grew silent with the exception of Jimmy's snoring.

But outside in the street, directly across from the hotel, Bob stood watching. He knew the companions were the only guests in the hotel at the moment so the lighted window was the one he wanted.

He waited until it was almost pitch dark on the street and the lanterns inside the room had been dimmed for more than an hour, then he turned and left. But he would be back, and with friends.

What happened to him at the saloon wasn't over in his mind, and when he was through this night, Watson and Jimmy would have their throats cut, Cindy would be his, and the other men could have Mary for a reward for helping him out.

As for Donaldson, he wasn't worried. He planned on keeping things in the hush-hush and the next morning there would be nothing in the room but a few patches of blood staining the walls and carpeting.

He knew Donaldson could give a shit what happened to a bunch of strangers, especially ones who'd pulled the crap the companions had at the saloon.

Oh, yes, once they were gone, Donaldson would forget about them and Bob would have fun with Cindy until he grew tired of her. Then he'd slit her throat and toss her in the ditch at the rear of the town, the mass grave where Donaldson's enemies usually ended up.

As he made his way through the darkened streets, other shadows were moving nearby as other townspeople headed to a fro, preparing to bed down for the night. He grinned widely in anticipation.

One more hour and he would have his vengeance...and a new piece of pussy to play with for the foreseeable future.

A little more than an hour later, Bob was back at the hotel again, standing across the street. Behind him were three more men, their faces familiar to anyone who had been at the saloon earlier that day. They were three of Donaldson's cronies, but they were always up for a little fun. They, too, were pissed about what happened today at the saloon and were looking forward to a little payback.

With Bob in the lead, the four men skulked across the street to the main doors of the hotel. Entering into the small lobby, the hotel manager's mouth dropped open at the sight of Bob and his henchmen. It was late and there should be no reason for any of the men to be in his hotel

Bob raised his left hand to his lips to silence the manager and raised his other hand to his throat, gesturing with his finger in a slicing manner, as if his finger was a knife and he was splitting his throat.

The warning was clear. The manager would shut his mouth or die. The manager nodded slowly, signifying he understood the gesture.

"I saw a light on in a window. Is that where they are?" Bob asked the manager.

The man nodded, pointing down the hallway.

"Key," Bob said.

The manager handed Bob the master key to open any room in the hotel.

Bob grinned malevolently as he took the key, then he waved his men onward, down the hallway and to the companions' room. As he moved, he pulled a long, nine inch knife from his back while the other men did the same. One man had a butcher's knife, another a cleaver, while the third carried a stiletto.

Bob wanted things to stay quiet. No guns. He needed this to be entirely covert.

Sneaking down the hall, he stopped when he reached the correct door while one of his men made sure the small lantern in the hallway was doused. It wouldn't do to open the door and let light spill inside the room.

Glancing to his men, he raised a finger to his lips, telling them to stay silent.

Then he turned back to the door and slid the key into the lock.

This is gonna be too easy, he thought as he slowly opened the door.

The door opened on greased hinges and Bob slipped into the room. The smell of peanut butter hung in the air which was mixed with the scent of gun oil.

He could see shapes on the bed and the floor, the one on the floor snoring rather loudly.

Good, it would cover the noise he and his men made as they got into position to strike. He was already planning on how he was going to rape the blonde while his men had fun with the brunette. And all the while, the two men would lie bleeding to death within a few feet. But then a gunshot filled the room, sounding louder in the small space, and sudden pain filled Bob's chest.

He was pounded back like a fist had slammed into his body and he stumbled into one of his men. In the gloom of the room, he just made out the shape of someone standing in the corner, the chair the person had been sitting in now pushed to the side, ignored.

Bob was about to yell to his men to attack or run, whatever no-tion came to mind first, when another shot struck him directly where his heart was, the bullet shredding the organ and killing him instantly. As his mind shut down, he registered another shot and felt warm blood splatter on his face as one of his men took a round to the head. Then the gloom of the hotel room was replaced by utter darkness as he stepped onto the last train west with a one way ticket.

Yells filled the room now as the last two men decided the plan was a bust and tried to escape. The first man spun and backpedaled while his buddy followed. No sooner did the second man turn to run then he was shoved forward by a round to the back, the force of the impact throwing him forward to catch the heels of his fellow attacker.

The other man tripped and cracked his head against the door frame, but it was only a glancing blow and he recovered and kept running. Another shot sounded, and the doorframe an inch from the man's left shoulder exploded into wooden splinters, but the man escaped unharmed.

By now all the companions were awake, Mary, Cindy and Jimmy with their guns in their hands, the weapons with them even in sleep.

But their vision was blurry from sleep and the room wreathed in shadows, there was no target to shoot at. Mary spun in the bed where she was next to Cindy and almost fired at a shape at the foot of the bed when a lantern came on, banishing the darkness, and she realized it was Henry.

Holding her fire, she looked around the room.

Everything happened so fast that Jimmy, Cindy or Mary hadn't managed to get up. Jimmy, on the floor was sitting up with wide eyes, completely taken off guard.

"What the hell is going on?" Jimmy yelled as he looked around and up at Henry.

Henry stepped away from the lit lantern and walked to Bob's bloody corpse, kicking the body with his foot. He did the same to the other two men and then turned to the others.

"We had visitors, that's what happened. Good thing I decided to stand watch."

Mary shifted in the bed and said. "But I thought we decided we didn't need one. If Donaldson wanted us dead he had his chance a dozen times. We all agreed we were as safe as we could be here."

"Maybe," Henry said. "But the truth is there's nowhere safe anymore, Mary. I just decided to watch over you guys. Why, you telling me I was wrong?"

She frowned. "Of course not."

Jimmy was on his feet now as well as Cindy, and he padded over to Bob's corpse and gazed down at the dead man. He was in nothing but his underwear and it was an odd sight, what with the .38 in his hand.

"Hey, it's the asshole from the bar. What the fuck's he doing here?" Jimmy asked as he knelt down and picked up the man's knife. He then went to the other two men to see they too had blades. "What the hell were these guys up to?"

"You mean other than trying to kill us in our sleep?" Cindy asked as she put on her shirt and then quickly slid into her pants. Mary was doing the same, feeling vulnerable.

Henry was fully dressed, right down to his boots, and he went to the door and peered out, careful in case there was someone waiting to take a shot at him. He could hear voices and a few yells. He would have company again soon, someone coming to investigate the gunshots in the middle of the night, no doubt.

Henry looked back to the others. "Jimmy, get dressed, and as for why they were here it doesn't matter. All that matters is they're dead and we aren't. But I missed one, he got away."

"So," Mary said. "What's he going to do? Complain to Donaldson that he broke in here and got stopped from killing us? Even Donaldson won't take his side for that."

"Maybe, but don't forget we're strangers here. And Donaldson already warned us once. Even though this isn't our doing, he still may use this as an excuse to…"

He didn't get to finish his sentence thanks to a voice cutting through the dead of night with the help of a bullhorn, followed by the sound of an engine. It was Donaldson and he didn't sound happy.

"*Attention in the hotel, you're under arrest for killing three of our people. You will come out with your hands up and surrender your weapons where you'll be tried in a court of law.*"

Jimmy ran to the window and peeked out the side of the curtain.

"Jesus Christ, there's got to be twenty men out there. How the hell did they get here so fast?"

Henry moved to the window and peered out too and he frowned deeply at what he saw. There were two squad cars and a pickup truck, and behind the vehicles had to be a dozen plus men. Some looked tired like they had been up all night while others looked wide awake. If he had to guess, he figured the escaped man had hightailed it to the saloon where Donaldson had been informed, probably with lies about what really happened. From there the constable gathered his men and got to the hotel.

The entire gathering had taken minutes with the saloon only a few blocks away. And then he saw Donaldson standing to the side of one of the squad cars, the man who'd gotten away next to him.

In the headlights of the car, Henry saw the man had a head wound and he guessed the shot that struck the doorframe must have sent some wooden splinters into the man's skull. Henry could only imagine what the man had told Donaldson, a pack of lies the constable wouldn't think twice about believing.

Cindy slid up next to Henry. "So, what are we gonna do? We're not going to surrender are we?"

"Hell, no," Henry said. "The only thing we got going for us right now is Donaldson knows we're well armed. We give up our guns and we're as good as dead."

"*You hear me, Watson? Give up or I'm coming in there, and when I do you're dead!*"

"Shit, we're already dead, and he knows it," Jimmy sneered.

He snuck another peek put the window and could see the men all had rifles and handguns. By the way they looked, they sure didn't seem like they were willing to settle this peacefully.

"Well, it doesn't hurt to try anyway," Henry said and went to the window. Opening the window he called out to Donaldson.

"What're the charges?"

The second Henry showed his face, a gunshot rang out and the frame an inch from Henry's face blew apart. Ducking down, he cured himself for being a fool, as the others dropped to the floor.

"*Cease fire, Cease fire! Who's the asshole that fired without my say so? Well?*"

A man in his late fifties raised his hand, a bashful look on his face.

Donaldson saw the man as he raised his hand and before the older man could do anything, Donaldson drew one of his Magnums and shot the man in the chest, sending him flying backwards to lay sprawled on the road, dead eyes staring at the night sky.

"No one fires with out my say so, dammit," Donaldson muttered as he holstered his gun. He raised the bullhorn. "*Sorry about that, Watson; the problem's been fixed. No one'll shoot again without my say so.*"

"Good to know," Henry mumbled as he snuck a peek through the window. He had a few small scratches on his face but nothing serious.

Deciding it was probably safe, but this time staying behind the window frame, Henry called out again.

"So, as I was saying, what're the charges?"

Donaldson confirmed with a few other men, including the attacker who had gotten away from the hotel room, and then he turned back and raised the bullhorn to his mouth.

"Murder, times three. You killed Bob, Watson. You have to answer for that. But I promise you that you'll get a fair trial? All of you."

Jimmy made a raspberry. "Now there's a load of bullshit if I ever heard one."

Henry ignored him and called back to Donaldson.

"How can it be murder when they attacked us? The room was locked and they broke in. We were simply defending ourselves."

"That's not the way I hear it, Watson. This is your last chance, come out or we're comin' in!"

"Give us a minute to talk about it!" Henry called back.

"Thirty seconds, that's it!"

Henry turned to the others and Mary was the one to ask the question on all their minds.

"What do we do?"

"We get the hell out of here, that's what," Henry replied. "We take the back way out and head for the wall at the opposite end of town. Once there, we should be able to climb it. It's to stop deaders not humans and it's to keep people out not in." He gestured to their gear. "Come on, we got twenty seconds and we're outta here."

A flurry of activity began in the room as each of the companions rushed to gather their gear.

Fifteen seconds later, everyone breathing hard from exertion, they were ready to go.

"Okay, Jimmy, you take the rear with that shotgun, you girls follow me," Henry said as he opened the door and peered outside. The hallway was empty, so he took a tentative step out of the room. His Glock swept the small hallway and then he waved the others onward.

Single file, they made their way to the back of the hotel where an unlit exit sign hung impotent over a metal door with a cross bar.

Henry stopped at the door and glanced to the others.

"See? Home free," he said and then pushed on the crossbar.

As the door swung open, he scanned the darkness, but so far it was quiet. From the side of the building, the glow of the red and blue lights of the squad cars could be seen and Henry felt like an escaped convict in a criminal drama. For just a second he thought back to his life before the dead began to walk and was amazed how different he was now. Deep inside, he was the same man, but now there was a well of strength he'd never known was within him.

"Okay, stick to the shadows and before you know it we'll be gone and can forget this damn town ever existed."

The girls nodded and Jimmy only grunted, then they began to creep out the door. It was as Jimmy was passing the doorway of the hotel that excited shouts rang out followed by gunshots. A round went so close to Jimmy's head he felt the air shift by its passing, and he dropped to the ground and rolled, coming up in a shooter's stance, the shotgun braced against his hip.

Flashes of gunfire told him where his assailants were and he let off two shots, the shotgun's wide barrage of death finding targets immediately. Next to him, Cindy did the same, firing a spray of rounds into the darkness with the M-16, a cry of pain her reward. Henry fired as well, shooting just a few inches above the muzzle flashes. He was rewarded by a grunt and a shape slumped over a trash can.

Mary didn't fire, she knew to try to carry on a firefight at the back of the hotel was a losing proposition and she yelled to the others to get back inside the hotel. Her foot caught the fire door just before it closed and saved them all from being trapped outside. Kicking the door open, she yelled above the cacophony of gunfire for Henry and the others to follow her.

Henry, hearing her voice through the din of gunfire, turned and saw her waving. Firing off three more rounds, he quickly began backing up, grabbing Cindy as he did so. The blonde was strafing the darkness in front of her, keeping the heads down of the hidden gunmen.

"Jimmy, let's go! Fall back!" Henry yelled.

Jimmy fired three more times and finally Henry's voice pierced the haze of battle. Stepping back, he ran to the door, a round ricocheting off the wall after it zipped through the side of his shirt. He yelped as the bullet grazed his flesh, but when he didn't feel a wet spot he knew he'd cheated death yet again.

Then they were back inside and Mary slammed the door closed just as a dozen rounds peppered its steel facade. None penetrated the metal and the companions breathed heavily as they took stock of their new predicament.

"Well, guys, that's didn't go as planned," Henry said as he leaned over and sucked in air.

"Bastards were waiting for us. Ambushed us good, too. That Donaldson's smarter than he looks," Jimmy said as he ejected spent shells and reloaded.

"Yeah, maybe," Henry added. He looked to each of his friends, his eyes scanning them for wounds. "Anyone hit?"

Cindy and Mary shook their heads and Jimmy shrugged.

"Got grazed on the side but it's barely a scratch. I'll live."

"Good," Henry said. "Okay, new plan, we get back to the room and figure out what the hell to do next. Come on."

They ran back down the hallway, their boots slapping the low pile carpeting.

"We killed some more of their people back there, Henry," Mary called out as she ran. "If we thought we had a chance for a fair trial that's gone now."

"Doesn't matter, Mary. There wouldn't have been a fair trial, it would have been staged. Donaldson owns this town. The trial would've just been for show, but the result would've been the same."

"So what are we gonna do now?" Jimmy asked as they reached the room again. His eyes studied the hallway, but this was the best place to be at the moment. He considered checking out the lobby and Henry shook his head.

"No, Jimmy, if they got the back covered then they sure as shit have the front covered. I don't like going back into our room, but at least from there we have a good line of sight to the front of the building." He turned to Mary. "You stay out here and keep an eye out for anyone. Someone shows their head, take it off, no questions, got it?"

Mary flicked her head curtly. "Got it, anyone pops up, I take them down, no mercy."

He squeezed her arm and smiled, then the three of them went back inside to see what was happening out front. Henry parted the curtain and could see there was a lot more activity now. Men were running back and forth and more guards had arrived, all armed with assorted firearms.

Saying things had gone from bad to worse was an understatement. He glanced over his shoulder at Bob's corpse lying silently on the carpet and wished the man was still alive so he could kill him again.

This was all because of that idiot trying something stupid in the middle of the night. Now Henry had a mess for them all and it was very possible he might not be able to get them out of it in one piece.

Looking back out to the street, his attention flicked to the left of Donaldson where a man had arrived with a large torch. Another man had a gas can with a spray nozzle on the end. Before he could look more intently, Donaldson's voice sounded with the help of the loudspeaker.

"Watson, you there!"

"Yeah, I'm here, what do you want?"

"I owe you for more blood now. You killed four of my men and wounded two more when you tried to escape. That was foolish, the building's surrounded."

Jimmy chuckled at Donaldson's words. "You'll never take me alive, coppers, see, yeah, yeah, I'll take you all with me, yeah, you dirty rats," he said in his best Jimmy Stewart voice.

"Knock it off, Jimmy, this is serious, this guy's not screwing around," Henry chastised him.

Jimmy looked dejected. "Yeah, Henry I know but shit, it's not like the first time something like this had happened to us. We'll figure a way out of it, right? Hey, you always come up with a plan."

Cindy piped in. "Yeah, Henry, Jimmy's right. Ever since I joined you guys you always figure a way to get us out of tight scrapes. You must have some idea what we can do."

Henry shook his head; there was nothing he could do. They were surrounded with a hell of a lot of firepower aimed at them and even if they somehow managed to slip the perimeter now set up, they still had to make their way through the town.

"Hey, Watson, you hear me! That was some fucked up shit you just pulled, now all bets are off. You murdered my men and now you and your friends are gonna pay!"

Henry turned back to the window. "You try anything like coming in here, Donaldson, and a lot more blood's gonna be spilled! You know the weapons we have. And you know we'll use them to defend ourselves. Tell you what, let us leave peacefully and we'll go and never return. Bob started all this shit and that's who you should be punishing. But he's dead so it's over. Those men in back tried to kill us, so we defended ourselves. This doesn't have to continue!"

"You're right, Watson, and I'm gonna fucking end it right now!" He turned to his men and raised his hand in the air, his fist filled with his Magnum. *"Fire! Take that fucking place apart!"*

Like a light switch had been thrown, every man and a few women began firing at the hotel, directly at the companions' window. Henry, Jimmy and Cindy dropped to the floor as the world became nothing but zinging rounds and shattering glass.

The pictures on the far wall were peppered with bullets before they were smashed to the floor. The wall took on the look of Swiss cheese as round after round pummeled the plaster. The noise was deafening and Mary stared in horror from the hallway. But then she had her own problems when three men popped up at the far end, trying to get to the room.

She spotted the first man before he saw her and she shot first, her slug catching the attacker in the chest and throwing him off his feet. He hit the wall and slid down to the floor, a red streak now spread across the wall from his body's passage.

The second man was halted in his tracks at the sight of his dead pal, but before he could turn and run, another of Mary's rounds found his head, blowing out the back of his skull and making his face an unrecognizable mass of meat and bone.

With two of the bodies slumped to the floor, the last man turned and dived back behind the corner where the hallway dog-legged to the right, just as another slug ricocheted off the corner, missing him by inches. Mary crawled into the doorway and held her watch, while behind her the room was being demolished.

Jimmy, on the floor with gritted teeth, yelled to Henry. "We can't let this shit happen, we need to defend ourselves!"

"Oh, yeah?" Henry replied. "Well then go right ahead and stick your head up and tell me when it's safe!"

"Fuck that, I was just saying…"

"Well then shut the hell up!" Henry retorted as he covered his head with his hands and rode out the bullet storm. The cacophony continued unabated for another minute and then seemed to slow down as the men outside began to reload. Cindy was the one to act, jumping up and sticking her M-16 out the window. Locking on to the squad car's headlights, she began to fire, spraying an entire clip in a matter of seconds.

The bullets walked across the squad car, blowing out the head-lights, and then climbing up the front windshield, shattering glass into a thousand pieces.

Then she shifted right, and as she went from left to right, she began riddling the bodies of men stupid enough to be standing out in the open. Bodies danced a jig as they were knocked off their feet to lay in unflattering poses, large bloody wounds in their torsos and upper legs.

Then Cindy's clip ran out and she ducked back down, but Henry, taking her cue, popped up and began dealing death himself, firing with his Glock. He picked his targets carefully, aiming for heads like he was so used to doing with the undead.

A man with a rifle was looking back and forth in panic and then his head snapped back, now with a third eye, the hole now weeping blood.

He fell away behind a car to never breathe again. Two more men received similar treatment, one man catching a round in the eye. The orb popped like a small balloon as the bullet entered his brain, then flew out the back of his skull, taking most of his brains with it.

He dropped to the ground to flop around like he was being electrocuted, but no one noticed, all too busy diving for cover.

By the time Henry was finished, four more men were down and dead, and when you added them to Cindy's target practice, more than half the posse was now out of the fight.

Hiding behind one of the squad cars, Donaldson was screaming at his men to return fire, but no one was listening.

Then Henry spotted the man with the gas can again standing next to the man with the torch and he shifted his aim, firing a second later at the gas can, the container erupting into a blazing fireball, the explosion killing the man with the torch instantly.

At first, no one knew what was happening, but when the man who'd held the gas can, now wreathed in fire, ran past the squad car and into the no man's land between the hotel and the squad cars, everyone saw him clearly.

His hair was gone, his eyes melting as he ran around screaming. But his shrieks only lasted a second or two as he sucked in the flames which cooked his lungs and boiled his insides.

Henry decided to put the man out of his misery and he fired one more shot, striking the burning man in the side of the head. The 9mm round entered the immolated man's melting left ear and exited out the right one, the smell of boiling, seared brains filling the night as the flames pushed back the darkness.

The man flipped to his side and lay still as the crackling of his flesh and clothing continued. One guard couldn't take the visceral image and he puked on his shoes.

Henry pulled back behind the window frame and nodded to Cindy, proud of her marksmanship.

"Great job, honey, that'll give 'em something to think about."

She smiled as she slammed in a fresh clip.

"What the hell was that all about?" Jimmy asked.

Henry gestured with his chin out the window. "A guy had a gas can and another one had a torch. I think they might have been planning on burning us out, like they did at that town a few months ago when Mary got us into some local trouble. Remember, the stoning?"

"Hey, I said I was sorry about that, Henry," Mary called from the door.

"I know, Mary, it's fine, I'm just saying, we need to get out of here fast. All they have to do is set this place on fire and we're screwed." Henry peeked out the window to see utter chaos. The squad cars looked like junked wrecks, their front tires flat, the windows shattered.

Donaldson was trying to get his men under control as most of them dealt with the wounded and dead. It looked like a war zone out there and Henry nodded, pleased. Whatever was going to happen next, there would be a brief lull while Donaldson got his act together.

He considered trying to shoot Donaldson. He could see the man's head bobbing around as he moved behind the squad cars and other men, but in the end it wouldn't matter whether the man was dead or not.

This had grown beyond just the constable. He needed to figure out a way to get the town back on his side, so they understood they'd all been duped by Donaldson and that the companions weren't at fault.

Then Henry spotted the man who had escaped the hotel room, the man who had been with Bob. That was the only person who truly knew what happened wasn't the companions' fault and that gave Henry an idea, one that was risky, but at the moment he was all out of ideas.

Then Jimmy pulled him from his musings.

"So, old man," Jimmy huffed, concern on his brow. "Got any ideas?"

Henry rubbed his chin, feeling the stubble there, then ran his hand over his face and across his hair. The hair was once a deep brown, but now it was mostly gray. It made him look a lot older than he was, but he wore his new hair color like a badge of honor.

"Yeah, actually I do, but you won't like it and I know I sure as hell don't. It's pretty desperate, but we don't have a lot of options right now."

Jimmy clapped his hands. "So, spill it, what is it?"

With a sigh, Henry turned to look at Cindy and Jimmy, and then to Mary who was peering around the door as she kept one eye on the room and the other on the hallway.

Then, with a lull in the shooting for the moment, he filled them in on his plan.

"Tyrell, what the fuck are you doing here?" Donaldson asked when he spotted me standing to the side, trying to see everything yet stay out of the way, and of course trying not to get shot.

"I'm here to help, sir," I said, but my words were ignored, Donaldson was already moving to check on something else.

Bastard, I thought. Serves him right for messing with Henry and his friends. I had heard what was happening and got my ass over to the hotel. From there I heard all about what the surviving man from the hotel fight said and how Bob was dead. I didn't believe it for a minute.

For one thing, how could Donaldson explain why Bob and two of his cronies were now dead inside Henry's room? Of course, he wouldn't even try. Donaldson was having his fun, at the expense of the companions and a lot of good townspeople.

Many of the town followed Donaldson, not wanting to believe the stories about him. It's not like I could blame these people, mind you. Donaldson may be an asshole, and he may make people disappear from time to time, but he had kept the town safe since the dead began to walk.

Still, he was a bastard.

The redolence of charred human flesh permeated the air, the man with the gasoline can still smoldering. His flesh had cracked in many places now, exposing the bright red of muscle and sinew beneath.

His mouth was curved into a rictus of death and his face was pretty much burned off. I arrived just as Henry put the dying man down, showing the mercy that Donaldson wouldn't have bothered with.

Then I heard Henry call out from the hotel window and every man on Donaldson's firing line went stiff as each turned to aim their guns at the hotel. I could see the facade around Henry's window and it was a bullet riddled mess. It looked like giant termites had gone amuck, eating into the wood of the building, as well as the brickwork that surrounded the window frame.

"Donaldson, you there?" Henry called out.

"Yeah, Watson, I'm here. You know you're dead when I get you, right? Fuck the trial. You're a dead man! All of you are!" The bullhorn was loud and I had to cover my ears before I moved away from Donaldson's side.

"Maybe, but like I said, you try and come in and more of your people are gonna die. How many have you lost so far? How many more want to die for what wasn't our doing? That asshole Bob broke into our room; they had knives. Somehow I highly doubt he and his buddies were coming in to kiss us goodnight!"

One of the men near Donaldson turned to look at him. "Is that true? Did Bob break into their room?"

"No, that's bullshit, John, now get back to your position and shut the fuck up!" Donaldson snapped.

John shook his head. "Not if what he says is true. Look, Donaldson, I'm not gonna die because of some vendetta you've got against these people."

Donaldson face grew hard. "Listen, John, get your ass back to your position or so help me I'll shoot you myself."

John didn't learn from when Donaldson shot the old man for firing without permission it seems and he stood defiant.

John shook his head. "Fuck you, Donaldson, I'm leaving, you can do this shit without me." The man turned his back on Donaldson and was about to walk away when a gunshot filled the street and John was thrown forward, his face smashing into the hood of a squad car. Gravity took over and he slid to the ground, dead.

There was a bloody hole in his back where Donaldson put the bullet, but the front of the man's chest was a gaping hole, the exit wound three times as large.

Donaldson looked to the rest of his men, not the least bit concerned that he'd just shot a man in the back; murdered him in cold blood.

"Anyone else want to leave?"

No one spoke; no one so much as shook their head. There was nothing but silence.

"Good, now everyone get ready, when I say it's time, we storm the place and take those fuckers down once and for all. This is my fucking town and anyone who doesn't agree can follow John to Hell!"

Donaldson looked at me and I swallowed hard, wondering if he was going to shoot me, too, but then he glanced away and I breathed a sigh of relief. I thanked God for small favors right then.

Henry called out again, his voice breaking the silence.

"Hey, Donaldson, you done playing with your people or what?"

"What do you want, Watson, there's nothing left to say! You're dead and that's it!"

"Oh, I don't know. The way I see it, we can settle this shit without anyone else dying. That is, if you think you're man enough!"

"What the fuck are you talking about?" Donaldson's voice replied, amplified by the bullhorn.

"Simple, we can shoot this out and more of your people are gonna die. And they know this is gonna happen. We got plenty of ammo and the guns to do it. Sure you'll get us eventually, but I promise you, we're gonna take a shitload of your town with us. Just check your casualties so far!"

This got many of the men talking as they waited near Donaldson. They'd seen many of their own gunned down tonight and for what real reason they still didn't know for sure.

Only Donaldson and his cronies kept them from leaving. John had tried and failed, paying with his life.

Many of them were already thinking thoughts of trying to slip away, but they knew once this crisis was over, Donaldson would find them and deal with them. He wouldn't kill everyone, as he needed men to guard the town, but there were many things worse than death.

"*So, Watson, what do have in mind?*" Donaldson asked, taking the bait Henry dangled.

"That's the simple part, Donaldson. To save any more bloodshed, I challenge you to a fight to the death. Just you and me. If I lose, then my people surrender with not one shot fired, but if I win, then we get to leave unharmed. Come on, Donaldson, only a pussy lets people fight for him, a man handles his shit by himself. So, what are ya, a man or a pussy? You're not gonna let more of your people die when you can settle this yourself, are ya? Seems to me if I was one of your people, I wouldn't take too kindly to you tossing my life away like it's worthless. Some leader you'd be then!"

Donaldson made an incredulous face, then raised the bullhorn to his mouth.

"That's not gonna happen, Watson. You can forget about that macho bullshit right now!"

But no sooner did Donaldson reply then some of the townspeople began to talk amongst themselves. Many cast wary glances at Donaldson and a few frowned deeply.

Donaldson returned their gazes and his mind began to work.

Damn that Watson, he'd placed him in a hell of a position. If he told Watson no, he was going to lose the fear of the townspeople. Watson's challenge would make him lose face with his men.

Though he didn't want to face Henry in battle, not that he was worried, mind you, he realized quickly he had no choice in the matter.

If he refused, he would lose his stranglehold on the town. No one would fear a man too afraid to fight. He would soon have men coming out of the woodwork, wanting to challenge him.

Every time he made an unpopular decision, he would find himself battling for his position again. He'd been maneuvered into a corner and there was now only one choice to make.

But he would have to make sure there was no chance he could lose, no, there was too much at stake for that to happen.

Turning, he called one of his men over and whispered into his ear. The man was one of Donaldson's trusted inner few and would do whatever was needed of him.

As Donaldson whispered, the man nodded, then picked up his rifle with a sniper's scope attached and jogged away.

"You're not really gonna do it, are ya, Boss?" One of his men asked from his side.

"Yeah, Bert, I have to. But it's not for Watson, it's to make sure the people of this town know I'm still in charge and not afraid of anything. Don't worry, I've already made sure of the outcome of this fight."

The man nodded, not understanding what Donaldson meant, but that didn't matter. Bert was a few gallons short of a full tank but followed orders without question, which was why Donaldson had him in his inner circle.

Donaldson glanced over his shoulder to see his man with the sniper's rifle was gone after rounding a nearby building which overlooked the street. Then, with a sneer on his lips, he raised the bullhorn again.

"Fine, Watson, I accept your challenge. Come out now without your weapons and no one will harm you. I'll meet you in the middle of the street! We'll do this now, no stalling! Any of my men see a weapon and they gun you down on the spot!"

"Fair enough, I'm coming out!" Henry yelled.

The townspeople began to murmur and a few nodded at Donaldson.

The constable eyed them back, then set his Magnums down on the hood of a car, said a few words to his men on what was going to happen and that they should be ready for what came next, and then strode out into the street to wait for Henry.

He knew many of the men talking to one another wouldn't be cheering him on and it was only his own cronies that protected him from feeling a gunshot to his back. No, his men would make sure no one got any ideas.

He'd made many enemies in town, more than he'd care to count, but he didn't care. To own power, to hold on to it, a man had to do things others found unpopular, and Donaldson liked the power he controlled, and if he had to kill to keep it, that was fine with him.

With hands empty, he slowed when he was in the middle of the street. Off to his right was the man who'd been set aflame, the acrid smell of the burned flesh tickling his nose. He squeezed his hands together as he prepared for the fight.

Though he preferred to let others handle the dirty work, he knew when this was over, and Watson was lying broken, bleeding and dead at his feet, the townspeople would never consider fucking with him again.

This would cement his authority for years to come.

He looked up when the front door of the hotel opened and Watson stepped out. Henry was unarmed, and if he was foolish enough not to be, one of Donaldson's men watching behind him would take Henry out immediately.

As Watson moved closer, Donaldson grinned widely.

This was gonna be good.

* * *

Henry slowed when he was a few feet from Donaldson, the entire town standing silent, waiting for what would come next.

"I didn't think you were man enough to face me," Henry said as he looked Donaldson up and down, sizing him up. The man was larger than him and had almost six inches of height over him. As far as brawn went, the fight's outcome didn't bode well for Henry.

If Henry showed he was worried, he hid it well. Truth be told, Henry wasn't worried. Unlike Donaldson, who'd been hiding in the town since the world fell apart, Henry had been on the road, fighting, killing and doing things some men would rather die than do. But he did these things to survive and he would continue to do so for as long as he sucked in breath.

Donaldson may be larger, but Henry was more experienced when it came to battling for one's life.

"You didn't give me much choice in the matter, Watson. If I refused I'd lose my standing in my town."

Henry nodded slowly. "Yeah, that's what I figured. Men like you, they don't fight their own battles, they send others to do it. I guess you're not a coward after all."

Donaldson grinned, taking the compliment. "No, Watson, I'm not and you're gonna find..."

He had to stop talking in mid-sentence because before he knew what was happening, Henry had sprung from what looked like a casual stance and he sent a right hook into his jaw, sending him flying backwards.

Stumbling away, Donaldson tried to fend off the savage attack, unused to the viciousness of the assault. Whatever he was expecting, he didn't expect this, but what he didn't know was that Henry wasn't interested in playing fair. This was a battle to the death, and whoever was left standing was the victor and how that person got there was irrelevant. Kicking, biting, scratching, whatever would do the job was fine with Henry.

In the law of the jungle, there were no *time-outs*; there was only life and death.

Henry followed up the first punch with one to Donaldson's kidneys, the man letting out a *whoosh* as his breath was forced out of him. But Henry was still moving and a left uppercut sent Donaldson's head rocking back, the man seeing the night sky.

Donaldson could hear people yelling, cheering, but who they were cheering for was unknown. Then he felt a blow to his throat that had him gasping for air. But this time Henry moved in close and Donaldson reached out and grappled with his attacker. Like a drunken, drowsy boxer, Donaldson hung all over Henry as he received repeated blows to his midsection.

Donaldson managed to sink a few blows in himself and Henry backed off, one scoring on his upper left eye. Breathing heavily, Donaldson tried to wipe the sweat from his brow with a shaking arm before the next attack came.

And he didn't have to wait long.

Henry ran at him and at the last second, he dropped to his knees and used his right leg to sweep Donaldson's legs out from under him. He went down hard, feeling the pavement beneath his back as Henry jumped on top of him, now raining blows down on his face and neck.

Panicking, Donaldson bucked under Henry, but the man lifted his butt and rode him like a bull, still slamming his fists into Donaldson's face.

But Donaldson grinned despite the pounding. Knowing he was losing under the onslaught of each blow, he raised his right hand into the air. To any onlookers it looked like a simple reaction to his beating, but to a shooter on a nearby roof overlooking the street, it was a signal.

Earlier, when Donaldson had sent the man away with the sniper's rifle, he gave the man strict instructions. If he raised his arm and it looked bad, that was the signal to take Henry out and to hell with the charade of fighting him.

Donaldson would deal with the townspeople later if that happened, but he had to live to do it.

So when the arm went up, the man on the roof lowered his eye to the scope and sighted Henry's chest in his sights.

His finger began to tense on the trigger, another quarter ounce of pressure all that was needed to send an explosive round into Henry's chest, killing him instantly.

But just before he finished squeezing the trigger, he suddenly gasped and began to twitch, his finger slipping out of the trigger guard. As the man laid bleeding and gurgling, another shape appeared behind him in the darkness from where it had snuck up on him unawares.

Cindy stood up and wiped her blade clean on the back of the man's shirt, the bubbling wound on the back of the man's neck, right over his spine, still squirting a dark liquid that seemed like ink in the gloom of the night.

Smiling, she pushed the man off the roof, the body tumbling to splatter like a sack of rotten peaches, and then knelt down and used the scope herself, this time to watch the fight in style. Swinging the scope back and forth, she checked the remaining rooftop, and seeing they were clear, she nodded to herself.

"It's all up to you now, Henry," she whispered as she peered through the scope again, wanting to see the fight play out and praying Henry would be the victor.

Down on the ground, Donaldson didn't understand why Henry wasn't dead and his heart skipped a beat when he realized his backup plan had failed.

But he wasn't out of the fight yet, and with a roar, he bucked his hips again, this time raising his left leg and getting it around Henry's waist. With a heave, the two men rolled to the side and Donaldson found himself free.

Rolling some more, he came up in a crouch, his face a bloody mess. He had trouble seeing thanks to the massive cuts on his brow, but he shook his head, red droplets cascading to the road between his feet.

Henry took this as an opportunity for a breather himself and he wiped his face with the end of his shirt, his jaw set tight as he stared at Donaldson.

"You fuck, I wasn't ready," Donaldson hissed.

"Fuck you, Constable; this isn't a school yard fight. It's to the death if you forgot."

Donaldson sneered as he reached down to his right side and raised the material of his pant leg.

"Oh, no, Watson, I didn't forget."

He withdrew his hand and now in his palm was a six inch, double-bladed knife, the sheath he'd pulled it from now clearly visible in the moonlight strapped to his upper ankle.

"Son of a bitch, you said no weapons," Henry hissed as he wiped his mouth.

Donaldson chuckled then, knowing he now had the winning hand. "Yeah, I did, didn't I."

He lunged from his crouch and slashed at Henry's stomach. Henry managed to dodge the blade, but not before he felt it bite the side of his left arm. It was a slight sting, but he knew he'd been tagged.

"Shit," Henry hissed.

Donaldson began moving to the left and right slowly as he moved closer to Henry.

"Shit it is, Watson. I'm gonna carve you up like a Thanksgiving turkey."

Henry didn't reply, but kept his eyes on the glinting blade, the now blood-stained tip reflecting what moonlight there was.

Donaldson moved in again, slashing at Henry's face and he almost tagged him again, but Henry managed to duck away. Each time Henry tried to go on the attack, he was driven back by the blade.

"What's the matter, tough guy? Lose your courage?" Donaldson needled as he chuckled. He wiped his brow again, his shirtsleeve now sopped in red, but he never took his eyes off Henry.

"Sooner or later I'm gonna getcha, its inevitable," Donaldson gloated.

Henry's mind spun in circles as he tried to figure out how to finish this without getting gutted. Donaldson had the longer reach, and with the knife, Henry was at a serious disadvantage.

But then an idea came to him and he went with it, all out of options. Before Donaldson knew what was happening, Henry jumped back a few feet and reached down and undid the laces on his boots. Before Donaldson could come at him, Henry had taken off his left boot and he danced away again.

"What the hell are you doing, Watson? Don't want to die with your boots on?"

Henry didn't reply, but danced away again and then took off his other boot when he had a free moment. Now he had both boots in his hands and he slid his right hand into the inside of the boot and the left one he held like a rock.

"So what, you're gonna throw them at me? Please, don't be pathetic. Just stand still and I'll make it quick," Donaldson said. "Well, maybe not that quick."

Henry was silent as he danced back and forth in his socks.

Donaldson swiped at Henry but his prey feinted away, Donaldson only cutting air.

To the townspeople watching, it must have been a ridiculous sight, watching Henry dancing in his stocking feet with one boot on his hand and the other cradled in his palm while Donaldson continually tried to cut him.

This went on for over three minutes, each time Donaldson lunged, Henry would backpedal away.

And then, Henry saw his chance. Whether tired or frustrated, Donaldson dropped his guard for a fraction of a second and Henry went into action.

Like a pitcher in the Majors, Henry wound up and threw the boot he was holding at Donaldson, the sole of the boot connecting with the man's nose.

There was a soft crack of cartilage and Donaldson howled in pain, but he knew better then to worry about his nose.

As he spun around, Henry was coming for him and Donaldson raised the knife, figuring if Watson was stupid enough to get in close, then he could gut the man like a fish and end this.

But as the knife went sideways to plant itself into Henry's midsection, the other boot was there, deflecting the blade like a shield.

The tip of the blade got stuck in the sole of the boot and Henry bent his wrist, sending both to fly away, the boot landing softly while the knife clattered across the pavement.

In what seemed like slow motion, both men stared into each other's eyes, then both turned as one and lunged for the knife, knowing this would be the only way to end this fight once and for all.

Both men reached it at the same time and fell to the road, their hands wrapping around the hilt as they struggled for dominance. Donaldson wound up on top and the blade disappeared between his and Henry's body as he pushed with all of his might.

Below him, with no leverage, Henry fought to keep the man off him, but he had no leverage and could feel the blade pressing on his chest.

Neither man could see the blade, the weapon shrouded in the folds of their clothes, and with a yell, Donaldson forced it down, Henry's eyes going wide in expectation of feeling the metal slide into his chest, slicing his heart in twain and killing him instantly.

But instead of feeling the kiss of the sharp tip, he felt the pressure from the hilt and he looked up into Donaldson's face as the man seemed to jerk from shock, the illumination more than enough to see the visage of utter disbelief now plastered there.

To the watchers of the fight, no one knew what was happening, and from their vantage point both men were still locked together with one on top of the other.

But Henry could see and feel what was happening, and as he stayed perfectly still, the pressure of the hilt pressing into his chest; he watched the light dim in Donaldson's eyes.

Blood began to seep out of Donaldson's mouth to drip onto the road an inch from Henry's face and that was enough for Henry to buck his hips and push the corpse off him as more blood seeped onto his shirt.

As Donaldson slid to the side to lie on his back, the knife protruding from his chest was apparent for all who could see. Coming to his knees, Henry sucked in a breath of air as he forced the little flashes of light to leave his vision.

And that was when Donaldson sat up and wrapped his hands around Henry's throat, trying to crush his larynx.

"I'll kill you," he rasped as he squeezed with whatever life remained in his dying body.

Like a zombie of the deadlands, Henry stared into the man's eyes, understanding Donaldson wasn't dead yet, but must have went into shock from the blade penetrating his chest.

Donaldson had the strength of three men now, his last wish on the planet Earth to take Henry to Hell with him.

Tensing his neck muscles to try and halt the assault, Henry tried to release the hands around his neck, but they were like a vise and he felt his vision growing dim as he began to black out.

"Die, you bastard," Donaldson hissed as he spit blood into Henry's face.

Henry let go of the hands, knowing they were too strong to get off in time and in a panic his left hand found the blade still protruding out of Donaldson's chest. Like a life line, he wrapped his palm around the hilt and then pushed deeper, twisting the blade and pulling it up, then down to Donaldson's groin, thus eviscerating the man.

As Donaldson's intestines began to seep out of the rip in his abdomen, the grip on Henry's neck began to grow less, and after another second Henry was able to bring his arms up under Donaldson arms and break free of the stranglehold.

Rolling free from the death grip, Henry came to a stop a few feet from Donaldson, who was on his knees, gasping for air.

Donaldson was staring at him, his arms still out like he was squeezing Henry's throat, and around his knees was a large pile of red and greasy intestines.

The constable gazed down, and seeing his organs lying on the road, reached down and picked them up, the coils sliding in and out of his hands like living eels.

He then began trying to force them back inside his stomach as tears of fear and pain slid down his cheeks, leaving runnels in the blood stuck there from the beating he'd received from Henry's fists.

Henry stood and watched the wretched man and then turned and walked over to one of Donaldson's men a few feet away, the man's mouth hanging open at the sight of his boss mortally wounded on the street. The man did nothing, just stared at Henry and then to Donaldson and back again, awestruck at the carnage before him.

Henry held out his right hand. "Give me your gun," he said coldly, his voice firm, the tone not to be disobeyed. "The man's already dead, he just doesn't know it."

Like a boy drilled from birth to obey his father, the man handed Henry his revolver.

Henry said nothing as he took the gun. He turned and walked back to Donaldson who was still crying and trying to force his slippery insides back into his torso. Bits of dirt, pieces of wood and other bits of debris were now stuck to the entrails as he tried to shove them back into his body.

Henry strode to Donaldson, cocking the gun as he moved, and when he was next to the man, he placed the gun to Donaldson's head and pulled the trigger, no warning, no nothing, he just fired.

Donaldson's head rocked to the side as half his head was blown off and the body slumped to the ground, the intestines now free to leave the body to spread out on the road like bloody snakes.

Henry cocked the revolver and turned to the gaping townspeople.

"You all heard what he agreed to! To the death! And that's what it was!

This shit's over! My friends and I don't have any arguments with the rest of you. I know you were only doing what he ordered. He's dead and so are his rules."

He eyed Donaldson's cronies warily for signs of trouble, but none of them made a move to argue with his words. They were now lost without their boss.

Henry looked to the left to see me coming up to him.

"Tyrell, good to see you again," Henry said.

"Yeah, Henry, me too," I replied and then I turned to look at the townspeople still watching silently. Donaldson's cronies still stood silent and I saw the man who had escaped the hotel room alive was now long gone.

None of Donaldson's cronies were leadership material; they were the ones who followed a leader.

"He's right," I said to everyone. "Henry just did what a lot of us have wanted to do for more than a year but didn't have the guts or were afraid of what might happen to us or our families if we failed. But it's done now. Donaldson is dead and we can either let his gang still control us or we can take this town back and make it what we want!" I looked at each face, making eye contact. "So, what are we gonna do?"

For a few seconds the men and women of my town looked at one another, each not knowing what to do and hoping one of them would have the will to be the first to act.

And then it happened.

Old Jasper was the one who made the first move. As he raised his rifle, he slapped the two men next to him on the shoulders and then pointed the muzzle of his gun right at Donaldson's cronies.

Donaldson's men were completely caught off guard and they lowered their guns and raised their hands, just as more of the townspeople did the same.

In seconds, Donaldson's men were disarmed and helpless. They were then herded into a corner of the street and guarded so they would stay out of trouble.

Suddenly, a cheer went up for Henry.

Behind Henry, the hotel door opened and Mary and Jimmy came out, then Cindy appeared from behind a nearby building, a rifle with a sniper's scope in her hand.

As the four companions reunited and Mary hugged Henry, another loud cheer went up for Henry Watson, the savior of our town. He'd done what no one in our town had the strength and courage to do; face and kill Donaldson.

Soon the townspeople were moving forward, the men already there and the new arrivals showing up after the news had run through the remaining townspeople; all of them wanting to slap Henry on the back and thank him.

It became a party atmosphere and soon hard liquor and home-brew arrived, after a few men ran to the saloon to grab a few full jugs.

Like Independence Day, the people celebrated, and as we drank and cheered Henry and his friends, Donaldson's body lay ignored, cooling on the road.

The corpse was barely noticed, people stepping around it, as death was nothing special to any of us in our new, harsh world, and as I accepted a mug of beer from a smiling woman, I laughed and clapped as well.

Though many may not understand how we felt that day, wondering how one man had managed to have us all under his thumb, I say go back to Hitler or Stalin or a hundred others for your answer. Once one man has solidified his power, it's hard for regular people to get out from under it.

But this day the little man won and it was all thanks to four strangers who wandered into our town seemingly by random chance.

The four companions stayed in our town for the next three days, finally relaxing after nearly three weeks on the road.

Henry's cut on his arm was treated and everyone in the town fussed over him, wanting him to be okay. All knew a simple infection could kill without discrimination. It wasn't like in the old days when you could just pop down the street to the drug store on the corner for some antibiotics and bandages.

Henry was treated like royalty and nothing he asked for was denied though he was modest with his requests.

Jimmy was the one who took advantage, asking for the best food and drink they had, and making a few jokes about how if he was single, he could have any single woman in the town. Of course this got him a few slaps and punches from Cindy who wasn't in the mood for Jimmy's particular sense of humor.

At the end of the three days, with the sun just touching the sky on a beautiful morning, the four friends gathered at the main gate, the corpses on the road from days ago now cleaned and disposed of, only a few dark bloodstains on the pavement left behind as proof the battle had happened.

"Are you sure you won't stay and be our constable?" This came from an old man in his sixties. He'd once been on the town council before Donaldson had taken over. There were others near him as well; almost half the town had come to see the companions off.

"Yeah, well, like I said before and all of the times you asked me. I'm flattered by the offer but staying here, in one place, isn't for me."

"But why? You could be happy here," came a woman's voice from behind the old man, a murmur from the crowd agreeing with her.

"Maybe, but from what I know of this country so far tells me no. From what I've seen, it doesn't pay to stay in one place for too long. That's how the deaders find you. Keep moving, that's what I'll do and so will my friends." He looked to Jimmy, Cindy and Mary next to him. "Right, guys?"

"Shit, yeah, Henry," Jimmy said. "Where you go, we go," he said with a grin as he wrapped his arms around Cindy and Mary who both elbowed him in the ribs. But it was playful and he was fine.

That's when I pushed my way through the crowd until I was standing to the left of Henry. He spotted me immediately and patted my arm.

"Hey, Tyrell, I was hoping I'd get to see you again before we headed out."

"What, you thought I'd let you leave without saying goodbye?" I asked as I shook Henry's hand. Jimmy smiled at me as did Mary and Cindy. We had become friends in the past few days, the group filling me in on their many adventures.

While I listened, I was amazed that these four people were still walking around and breathing.

"Well, I hoped not, anyway," Henry added.

I smiled too, but it was one of loss as I didn't want them to leave, but knew I couldn't stop them. They weren't from my town or any other. They had the wanderer's spirit and would continue to have it until they found whatever they were searching for.

"We're all going to miss you guys, you certainly spiced things up since you arrived," I told them.

"Yeah," Jimmy quipped, "we have a tendency to do that."

There were a few more goodbyes and a little small talk and then Henry turned and pointed to the gate, the guard on the wall above opening it.

Henry repositioned his heavy backpack, as did Jimmy, Mary and Cindy, the packs full of supplies and ammunition from our supplies.

It wasn't much, but it would get them more than halfway to where they were going...wherever that may be.

With one last wave, Henry walked out of the gate, his friends right behind him.

He only went a few dozen yards and then he left the road, traveling overland to avoid the possibility of walking into a congestion of the undead or possible raiders who would prey on the empty highways.

As the rest of the townspeople and myself watched Henry and his group reach the rise on the landscape, I saw him stop one last time.

I noticed his panga was in his hand now. He'd been using it to slap and slice away some of the wild brush near his legs to clear a walking path for the others.

He turned around to face me and the people near me and he raised the panga over his head, the rising sun turning his body into a silhouette.

As he stood there, his three friends by his side, he cut a stirring picture of something from the olden days, back when man survived by his will, the weapons he carried, and the strength in his arms alone.

He shook the panga one time over his head like he was waving to us and then lowered it. Without another glance to us, he turned away, the four of them walking down the incline where they were quickly lost from sight.

I stood there for more than an hour, long after the rest of the townspeople had moved on to return to their mundane lives of survival, and I wondered what it would be like to have been given the opportunity to have joined Henry and his team.

What would it be like travel the deadlands in search of adventure, hoping over the next hill was something better than what we all now had to settle for.

I let myself dream for about what ifs for a while and then I shook my head and came back to reality

That life wasn't for me. My life was here, with my family and the people of this town.

And I know that was where I would stay.

Now its ten years later, and though the dead are still around, they're becoming fewer and fewer between sightings. The ramshackle wall we once had protecting our town is now made of solid concrete, ten feet high. And while the undead are more of a nuisance now, the cannibals and raiders more than keep life interesting.

I'm almost thirty now and I've inherited the position of constable from my predecessor, who decided to retire after a close call at the saloon. A bar fight went bad and the former constable almost lost his life.

He told me the job was for the young and as I was just the right age and had been a prominent man in the community, the job was mine if I wanted it.

Of course I took it, even if I may not have wanted it at the time. But I had vowed the day Henry saved my life to make sure that second chance I was given was used for something good.

And I can't think of anything better than to watch over the people I call family, all seven hundred and twenty of them. Will be twenty-one in a few days as Peggy Sue Williams is about to give birth.

So while life is simpler now, it's still filled with hardship and stress, only of a different sort.

I'm writing this all down so future generations can know why our town was able to thrive as it did; all because one man by the name of Henry Watson arrived to save us from ourselves.

He showed us that true courage comes from within, and though you may be filled with fear, the fear must be ignored to overcome the evil that threatens to take us all back to Hell with it.

So I'm the constable now and I run this town in the memory of Henry Watson and his fellow warriors of the deadlands, and I honor their memory and what they stood for every day.

Sometimes, late at night, when the moon is high, and my wife and kids are asleep, I come out to my porch and I have myself a nice sit with a warm beer in my hand, and I gaze off into the star-dappled night sky.

When I do, I can't help but wonder what happened to Henry Watson.

Was he still alive out there somewhere after ten long years? Was he still fighting the cruel and unjust and leaving the world just a little bit cleaner than how he'd found it? Or was he dead, or worse, now walking around as one of them.

I guess in the end, it doesn't really matter, for each of us is fleeting on this planet we call Earth and only our memory of the deeds we do by changing others lives for the better will live on forever.

That's all any of us can hope for.

HOMEWARD BOUND

"Are you sure you want to do this, Henry? We can leave right now."

Henry Watson barely heard Sue's words, as he stood in the driveway that once upon a time belonged to his home. Behind him were Jimmy, Cindy, Mary and Raven.

No one spoke, no one moved, each feeling the sorrow and grief hanging in the air. Henry gave it off in droves, his broad shoulders now sagging with the weight of his past.

"Henry?" Sue Anders asked again.

"Huh?" Henry blinked and seemed to snap out of whatever fugue state he'd been in. So many memories, so many stories of his life were here. A life shattered completely the day the dead began to walk.

"I said you don't have to do this," Sue repeated.

Henry wiped his hand over his face, and the single tear that had appeared in the corner of his right eye was brushed away. No one saw it and he'd be damned if he was going to tell them.

Sue reached out and touched his arm and she felt him tense. Over the past year, they had become close as two lovers could be.

But no matter how much Henry told her he cared for her, she knew his heart still belonged to his late wife.

To Emily.

"Tick tock, Henry, we can't stand out here all day," Jimmy Cooper said, breaking the moment. "More deaders are sure to pop up the longer we're out here."

"Jimmy, hush," Cindy Jansen hissed, knowing her boyfriend was putting his foot in his mouth...again.

Mary Roberts stepped up to Henry's side and touched his arm. "Jimmy's timing is bad as usual, but he has a point. We can't stand out here forever." Her tone was soft, consoling.

Henry squared his shoulders and stood taller. He was a few inches shy of six feet but his presence made up for any lack of height.

He was a powerful man, all muscle, with once brown hair turned ash color thanks to graying in all the right places. At one time, he'd carried a paunch like most middle-aged men, but after years of living in a zombie wasteland, his body had grown hard, as did his mind. The paunch was long gone.

On his right hip his trusty sixteen inch panga rode in its leather sheath and his Glock 9mm was in its holster. Slung over his shoulder was a .22 hunting rifle.

He'd traded for it in the last town, and though not powerful, it could still put a zombie down if the shot was well placed. He preferred to use the rifle for hunting game, the lower caliber helping with not pulverizing the kill and thus leaving something to actually eat.

"I'm fine, Mary, Sue, really. It's a lot to take in, I admit it." Henry turned to look at them, making eye contact with each one. Cindy smiled when they met gazes and Raven only nodded. "Okay, I'm going in, I won't be long."

His eyes drifted from his companions to the street around him. Next to the driveway he could see the bones of his neighbor, Charlie. A little less than two years ago, Henry had shot the man in the head when Charlie had come stumbling out of the backyard as a zombie.

It seemed like a lifetime ago—because it was.

The man Henry was now was a far cry from who he once was.

A low moan came to the group and a zombie appeared, shuffling out from the side of a house three doors down. A second later another arrived, followed by three more.

Henry watched the five ghouls stumble towards the companions, and when he was sure there were only five, he tapped Jimmy on the arm. "Can you handle them?"

Jimmy sneered as if he'd been asked to count to five. "You have to ask? Yeah, old man, I think we can handle five deaders by ourselves."

Mary nodded. "Jimmy's right. We have this under control. Are you going inside still?"

"Yes, all right, damn it. I'm going," he said, and with a squeeze of Sue's hand and after receiving a kiss on the cheek from her for support, he began walking to his home, where if nothing had changed, the corpse of his wife was still lying on the kitchen floor.

Jimmy watched Henry walk away from the group, and when the man disappeared inside his house, he turned to face the others. "Okay, Mary and Cindy, you're with me. Sue, you stay here with Raven and keep watch. Make sure nothing pops up and bites our asses off."

"Okay," Sue said.

Raven wasn't happy about it. "I want to come, too, kill some of them fuckers." She flexed her fingers. Her fingernails were long and had been filed so they were razor sharp. They sliced through flesh as if it was paper.

"Next time, Raven," Jimmy said. "Just hang out here and make sure we don't get surrounded, all right?" He lowered his voice so only she could hear and said, "And keep an eye on Sue. You know she needs protecting."

"What are you two talking about?" Sue asked. "Did I hear my name?"

"Nothing, Sue, it's nothing," Jimmy said with a wide smile. It was the smile Henry called his 'wise ass' smile.

"Jimmy," Cindy called. "They're getting closer." She had her M-16 raised and was tracking the zombies, though she knew not to fire unless there was no choice. One gunshot would be all it would take to have every zombie in a mile radius on their asses.

Jimmy looked at Raven, his eyes locking onto hers. "We good?"

Raven nodded, though she wore a deep frown. She hated sitting on the sidelines when there were zombies to be killed.

Jimmy turned and jogged over to Mary and Cindy, who were both watching the ghouls carefully. Two more had popped up, bringing the number to seven, but the three companions weren't worried.

After two years of surviving in a dead world, they had become proficient in killing the living dead. Where once the sight of a walking dead man would have filled them with shock, now it was just par for the course, a daily chore that needed to be addressed.

Jimmy scanned the neighborhood as the zombies moved closer. He saw two images of his surroundings. The first was the true one, where homes were dilapidated from two years of neglect.

Weeds grew out of rain gutters, front doors hung open, and windows were broken, once manicured lawns now covered in waist-high grass. It looked like a Third World country or a better analogy was that it looked like a post apocalyptic landscape.

The second image was from his past, back before the dead walked, when he used to live on this street. Back then he'd been a no-good teenager with a crappy job and a pot habit. The two interspersed in his head as he blinked the latter image away and only let reality shine through.

The past was dead, and possibly so was the future, but the present was alive and well and he aimed to keep it that way.

Jimmy took a step forward so that Cindy was on his right and Mary his left and a foot behind him. He reached down and touched his Bowie hunting knife, making sure it was there. "Okay, ladies, let's kick some deader ass." He raised his shotgun, ready to use it like a bludgeon.

"Right behind you, lover," Cindy said with a grin as she spun her rifle around so she could use the butt as a club. Mary bent over and picked up a long tree branch. She braced it against the ground and used her foot to crack it in half.

She came up holding a four foot long limb, about three inches in circumference. More like a spear than a club, she waved it back and forth. On her hip was her .38, but she would only use it if there was no choice. She knew without a doubt there were ghouls in almost every house, and if enough noise was made, they too, would venture outside into the daylight.

Walking as a group, the three warriors advanced on the shambling zombies.

Henry entered his home via the front door. As he stepped inside, his nose twitched from the odor of decay, and of bodies long since rotted to dust. But the odor was old—months if not years.

He began to have second thoughts about what he was doing.

It hadn't been planned, this return home, but when the companions had found themselves in the Midwest once more and within a hundred miles of here, and in a working vehicle with enough fuel, he knew the time was right for a visit to where it had all started. Jimmy had agreed, as this had been his home, too. Mary had lived in the area also but she didn't truly call it home. She's been raised in California.

As he moved deeper into his house, he stopped in the living room. His eyes roamed over the furniture, the television, now smashed and on its side on the floor, and the wallpaper, now peeling.

Someone had been through here over the past two years, it was evident everywhere he looked. The couch had been set on fire and then doused, and he wondered if some drifter had been smoking and had fallen asleep.

The carpet had multiple stains on it, urine no doubt, and as he investigated further, he found a dried pile of human waste behind his easy chair.

Evidently, someone didn't feel it was worth using the bathroom but had taken a dump right there on the floor before moving on. He could see the reasoning, though skewed. The person wouldn't be returning and so could have cared less how they left the house upon leaving.

Anger rose in him at the person who had desecrated his home. He knew he shouldn't feel this way, that this place was no different than the hundreds he'd gone through himself, but still...this house was different.

This house was *his*.

Or had been...once upon a time.

The stairs leading to the second floor were off to his right and he slowly climbed them. His hand was on the hilt of his panga, the sixteen inch blade razor sharp and ready for battle. But his nose told him anyone or thing that had been there was long gone.

Entering his bedroom, his eyes fell on the bed, the window overlooking the street, the bureau where he once stored his clothes. All the drawers were pulled out and what few remaining items of clothing were scattered about.

He picked up a black sock, seeing the hole in the toe, remembering getting grief for wearing it with the hole. Where the other one was he didn't know. He remembered this particular sock fondly. When he'd worn the pair, his toe would jut out like a worm peeking out of the dirt. Emily would tease him about it but he said he would buy a new pair when the ones he wore were truly not worth wearing anymore.

Emily.

As he looked around his bedroom, signs of her were everywhere. Her clothing was on the floor, her hairbrush lying in the middle of the bed. Evidently someone hadn't wanted to take it with them.

He went to the bathroom across the hall. The door was closed. Ready in case there was something waiting within, he pushed the door open slowly. All he was greeted with was the redolence of old human waste. He quickly closed the door again. Well, at least someone had used the bathroom for its intended purpose, even if there was no way to flush due to no water pressure.

There was another bedroom at the end of the hallway, the door closed. He and Emily had never had children, so the extra room had never become a nursery, but had ended up a storeroom. After finding nothing in the house thus far, Henry's guard was down, something he would have chastised one of the others in his group for. In a world where the dead walked, only constant vigilance kept a man alive.

It was as he reached for the doorknob, turned it, and pushed the door open that at the same time, the odor of death came to him. Sickly sweet, the smell of a rotting body was something a person never forgot once experiencing.

As the door swung open, a rotting face appeared in the doorway.

Henry's eyes went right to the face, or what was left of it. The left side was all but missing, the white of bone glistening in the wan light of the room. The right side had flesh remaining, but it looked like melting wax, the skin seeming to slough off the cheekbone.

There was only one remaining eye, and the dull orb was on the same side as the drooping flesh. Hair was sparse on the skull, a comb-over now sticking up, pus and other unidentifiable fluids stuck to the follicles, making it look like the worst hair gel in the history of gels had been lathered on the scalp.

The clothing wasn't much better. A tattered, plaid shirt that was stuck to the torso in all the wrong places, thanks to more bodily fluids, and a pair of white slacks now so filthy with blood, excrement and vomit, that they were basically black.

All this Henry saw in an instant as the zombie reached out to grab him, wanting to finally feed after being trapped for so long. It had stumbled into the room more than a year ago and an arrant breeze had slammed the door closed. Too stupid to know how to open it, the room had become the ghoul's prison...till now.

The zombie came stumbling out of the room, arms at shoulder height, hands already preparing to grab Henry, its mouth open wide in anticipation of tasting human flesh.

Though the ghoul was a surprise, in an instant Henry raised his left boot and kicked it back inside the room. The zombie was thrown backward, the back of its legs hitting a box of Christmas decorations to spill over it and drop down on its ass.

It was comical the way it fell, like a toddler who didn't understand why he had fallen. Henry was into the room right behind the zombie, and as the ghoul looked up at Henry, the eyes caught the reflection of steel in the gloom.

The panga came down and to the side from a high arc, taking the head clean off the rotting shoulders. Brittle bone and tendons were no match for the keen blade, and the head soared off to roll across the floor, coming to a stop by a pile of old clothes Emily had stored, though she knew Henry had wanted them donated to Goodwill.

Something black, that had once been blood, spurted fitfully out of the neck stump of the corpse before the body toppled onto its side, its arms and legs twitching in slow spasms as whatever nerve receptors shut down.

Walking over to the severed head, Henry looked down to see the eyes were still moving, the jaw working back and forth, the tongue flicking at the air between yellow teeth. No moans issued from the open mouth, as with no lungs, no air, it was impossible. Henry raised his boot over the head, and was about to bring it down and crush the foul thing when he stopped and lowered his foot. He didn't really feel like getting zombie gunk on his boot, so instead, he pulled an old coat from the clothing pile and tossed it onto the head. Turning, he walked out of the room, closing the door behind him.

On the floor, the coat rippled slightly as the jaw on the decapitated head still moved.

Henry walked down the hall and to the stairs, then with a long sigh, did what he'd been putting off since entering the home.

He went to the kitchen to see his dead wife.

Jimmy was the first to go into action, taking down a zombie with little energy. It had been female in life but in death was nothing but a relic. The skin was withered to the consistency of parchment, the hair a frazzled mess filled with crawling insects. Even a spider had made a nest there, enjoying the excellent feeding ground.

The nest was shattered when Jimmy's shotgun cracked the skull in two and the zombie dropped to the ground, dead for good. Gray brain matter spilled out of the gash in the zombie's head to gleam in the sunlight.

Laughing at the kill, Jimmy jumped over the fallen body and ran at the next one in line, a zombified construction worker, complete with hard hat still on its head and a tool belt filled with tools still on its waist.

The zombie towered over Jimmy by more than a foot, and as the young warrior swallowed hard, he wondered if this ghoul was a match for him.

Meanwhile, Cindy and Mary went to the next zombie in line, the two women working as a team. The first zombie was clearly male, thanks to the bald head and bathrobe that was untied, exposing the ghoul's nakedness to both women. The zombie's penis and testicles swayed back and forth with each step the creature made, and when Mary and Cindy were no more than a foot away, the genitalia finally gave up the ghost and dropped off, the skin rotted to the point it couldn't support the weight.

"Oh wow, that's gonna put me off sex for the next year," Mary said, her lip curled up in disgust. The zombie ignored its missing member, stepped on it, and as a testicle was crushed like the stomach of a friend clam, oozing out the sides, the dead man came forward, now a eunuch.

Cindy merely chuckled and used her right leg to sweep it across the dead man's ankles, thus knocking the zombie over. The ghoul landed face first, its nose flattening, the forehead cracking from the impact. Cindy brought her rifle down on the back of its skull, right where the spine was. The blow snapped the neck like a twig and the zombie stopped moving.

"Next," Cindy grinned as she looked up. But she'd grown lazy and another zombie was coming up right behind her, its mouth wide in anticipation of a kill. Mary saw the ghoul and knew she was too far away to reach the zombie, but then realized she didn't have to be. "Duck!" she ordered Cindy, who didn't hesitate, the two trusting each other implicitly after dozens of battles together.

Cindy dropped to all fours, feeling vulnerable but relying on her partner, and when she looked up, she saw Mary throw the tree branch she held like a spear. The projectile zipped through the air, and a second later, impaled the zombie behind Cindy in the center of its chest. The ghoul stumbled backwards, its hands reaching for the protuberance in its torso.

Cindy swing a foot out and connected with the zombie's left knee, snapping it in half. One legged, the ghoul dropped to the ground, only the spear preventing it from falling over. It leaned against the pole for a brief moment, and then began to slide down it, leaving pus and gore on the spear as the body came to rest on the pavement.

"Thanks, Mary," Cindy said as she stood up.

"Glad to help," Mary grinned as she scanned the street for another weapon. The tree branch was covered in gore and she'd be dammed if she would use it now. Her eyes spotted a hubcap in the gutter, and after tipping it upside down so that mud and debris fell out of the concave side, she hefted it, satisfied with its weight. And just in time. Turning at the sound of scuffling feet, a dead woman in a tattered power suit reached for her. Mary used the hubcap as a muzzle and jammed it into the dead woman's mouth.

Rotting teeth clamped on the metal and a dull clank was heard. Holding the ghoul at bay with one hand, Mary drew her .38 and placed it against the woman's forehead.

With the muzzle pressed tightly to muffle the report, she squeezed the trigger, sending the ghoul's brains out the back of her head. The body dropped to the ground, immobile.

Cindy joined Mary as she retreated from the last three zombies, Jimmy joining them a second later.

"Three more to go," Jimmy said. He'd taken the construction worker out easily, and had been a little disappointed there hadn't been more of a fight.

"How do you want to do this?" Cindy asked.

"Blitz 'em," he replied, and with a look at both women to make sure they were on board, the three deadlands warriors charged the last three zombies, weapons raised high.

It was over in seconds. Cindy drop-kicked a zombie and crushed its skull, Jimmy punched one in the face and then swung around behind it, grabbed it by the head, and twisted, snapping the neck and spine, while Mary kicked the last in the right knee, using Cindy's previous move.

When the zombie fell to the street, Mary kicked it in the face, dislocating its jaw, then stomped on the face until the zombie was dead.

With all three breathing heavily from the skirmish, they returned to Raven and Sue.

"What's all this?" Jimmy asked upon spotting four bodies sprawled around Sue and Raven's location. Each zombie had been taken out cleanly and quickly.

Raven shrugged. "Nothing I couldn't handle," she said.

Jimmy nodded, knowing she wasn't lying. Raven was a hell of a fighter. One day, he hoped she might talk about her past but so far she hadn't said a word, despite him trying to get her to open up.

"Is Henry still in there?" Jimmy asked Sue.

"Yes. Should we check on him?" she asked.

Jimmy shook his head. "Nah. He said he wanted to be alone. I think it's best to honor his wish." He gazed down the street to his own house.

When they'd first arrived on the street, he'd decided he wasn't going to visit it. Too many bad memories from the last time he'd been inside there, but as he waited for Henry, he felt a nudge to do just that. Finally, he turned to Cindy and said, "I think I'm gonna go check out my house. After all, this might be the last time I ever get the chance."

"You want company?" Cindy asked.

Jimmy considered her offer and nodded, "Sure, that would be great." He looked at Mary and said, "You'll be okay here?"

"Sure. I'm fine. I'll wait with Raven and Sue for Henry. If he comes out early before you get back, we'll come and get you."

Jimmy waved and he and Cindy walked away, crossing the street, side by side the entire time. Jimmy was quiet, more so than normal, and Cindy could only imagine what was going through his head.

When they arrived at the walkway leading to the house, Cindy reached out and touched his arm. "You okay?"

At first he didn't answer, then he seemed to remember she was with him. He turned his head and nodded. "Yeah, I'm okay. It's just...well, the last time I was here it was pretty fucked up. I found my dad on top of my mom. He was eating her. I had to kill him."*

"Oh, Jimmy, I'm so sorry," she whispered.

He shrugged. "I'll be fine. Come on, let's get this done." He walked up the path to the front door, Cindy right behind him.

The door was unlocked and he pushed it open, then waited to make sure the home was empty.

He sniffed, trying to detect any unwelcome guests, but the odor of death was old, diluted from time. Something had died here, but it had been a long time ago.

With his shotgun leveled and his finger on the trigger, he entered his house. Behind him, Cindy slowly closed the door, not wanting anything to come in and attack them.

Jimmy didn't waste a lot of time walking around, but headed straight for the den in the back of the house. His ears searched for sounds other than his or Cindy's but the house was silent.

* See Deadwater Expanded Edition

As he passed through the kitchen, he saw every cabinet and drawer had been opened and pulled out, the ransacked room showing that others had been here in the past.

His feet crunched on broken dishes and bits of wood. A bag of sugar had been torn open at one time and ants were still busy working on the pile and had been for quite some time.

When he entered the den, he looked down and saw what he expected. The TV was still on the floor and under it was the crushed body of his father. His mother's corpse was in the corner, now nothing but skin and bones.

Tears welled up in his eyes as he stared at the remnants of his parents. Cindy touched his hand and he jumped at the feeling. "Is that your..." she began.

"Yeah, that's them." He sniffed, not wanting to cry, wanting to maintain control. "I didn't think it would get to me this way, you know? I thought I could handle it. Shit, I can't imagine how Henry is dealing with seeing his wife. Especially after he had to kill her the way he did."

Cindy said nothing. There wasn't really anything to say. Jimmy stood at the doorway for a full five minutes, Cindy by his side, then he finally snapped out of it.

Wiping his eyes with the back of his sleeve, he stood taller, squared his shoulders, and turned around. "Come on, I should see if there's anything in my bedroom worth taking. Maybe some of my old clothes are still there." He sighed. "I think I've had enough of going down Memory Lane for the time being."

Together, the couple walked back into the center of the house and to Jimmy's bedroom off the living room, leaving the two corpses alone once more.

Henry stood in the kitchen, looking down at what was once his wife. Memories of what had happened two years ago came flooding back, causing tears to well up in his eyes. He felt his legs go weak and he had to lean against the counter for support.

The same cast-iron frying pan that he'd used to crush his wife's skull in was still on the floor, her head so destroyed he wouldn't have known it was her if he hadn't been the one to put her down.

When she was alive, she'd been healthy, her body full with curves where they should be, despite her age of over forty. But after two years of rotting, the body was no more than a skeleton, a pile of bleached bones, with bits of material from the bathrobe she was wearing.

The shattered teacup was still strewn across the floor and their dead cat was now nothing but a dried-out husk in the corner. He thought back to when he'd first entered the kitchen to see Emily hunched over something as she sat at the table. He remembered the horror when she looked up and he saw her face covered in blood, the carcass of their cat on the table before her, its insides torn out and more than half of it in her mouth.

As he looked down at the skeletal corpse, he realized coming back here was a terrible mistake. He had made peace with what he had done to her, and coming back here now did nothing but stir up memories that were better left alone, better left buried deep in the ground where they could never see the light of day again.

The past was dead and there was only the present to live for, as even the future was trepidatious. Sue was waiting outside for him. She was his wife now, and this house and his dead wife and any possessions within, were now nothing but ghosts.

Turning, he walked into the living room and picked up a blanket that had been tossed haphazardly onto the floor by some unknown looter. Picking it up, he carried it back into the kitchen and knelt down before the corpse.

"I'm so sorry, Emily." He wiped the tears from his eyes. "I'm so sorry things turned out this way. It's not fair. To you, to me, to all of the world." He covered her body with the blanket, his eyes turning away from the dried gore on the cabinet from where her brains had slid down so long ago. Standing up, he sucked in a deep breath.

His eyes went to the doorway to the garage, the door hanging open. He could see the desiccated bodies lying on the cold floor and in the entryway from where they'd been put down before he, Jimmy and Mary had made their escape in his minivan.

He squeezed his eyes closed, and wiped his face clean with his hands. When he opened them and took his hand away, the firm jaw and cold eyes had returned, and the emotions he'd been feeling were now buried deeply, where they should have stayed.

Looking left and right, as he took in the house where he had once made his life, he now knew what he had to do to cleanse himself of the past once and for all.

Mary tapped her foot impatiently as she waited for Henry, Jimmy and Cindy to return from their little trip down Memory Lane.

"Where the hell are they?" she asked no one in particular.

Sue patted Mary's shoulder. "I'm sure they'll be out soon. I can imagine it's hard revisiting the past like this. I was surprised when Henry wanted to come here."

"I know what you mean," Mary said. "I was a bit surprised, too. We've all been through so much, to then come back here...well, I know I don't feel the need to go to my apartment. Besides, my true home is in California and when we were there a while back the last thing I wanted to do was ask Henry to follow me there. I know my parents are dead, they must be."

Sue didn't reply, she just stared at Henry's house.

Mary stepped away from Sue and said, "Look, I'm gonna go for a walk." Sue looked like she was going to protest and Mary held up a hand to stop her. "Don't worry, I'll be close."

"Shout if you need us," Raven called. She was sitting on the curb, inspecting her nails and trying to get any bits of flesh or blood that had gotten under them.

"I will," Mary replied as she wandered away.

She moved slowly, and drew her .38 just in case a zombie popped up from behind a car or an overgrown shrub. Her eyes scanned the neighborhood and she thought back to how it had looked that day when she, Jimmy and Henry had come here to gather supplies and take Henry's minivan.

Looking back, it seemed like another lifetime.

There was a house to her left, the property surrounded by tall shrubs. Once manicured, now they were a mess of branches and leaves, the tall grass coming to her knees before it had fallen over on itself.

The house was familiar, and as she thought back, she remembered why. This had been the house that she'd found a once pregnant woman on the lawn, and when she had peered over the bushes, had found that the woman had died and the baby in her stomach had become one of the undead, and had eaten its way out of the mother's stomach.

Back then, she hadn't been as hard as she was now, and the sight had frightened her terribly. Jimmy had come to her aid, killing the baby and taking her back to join Henry.

Now, as she stood before the home and the shrubbery hiding where the body once was, she couldn't help but let her curiosity lead her back to that same spot.

As she walked, her eyes darted back and forth, making sure there were no other undead in the area. So far it was quiet, though that could change at any moment.

She approached the shrubs warily, and found a spot where the branches weren't as thick.

Moving to the spot, she slowly leaned over to peer into the overgrown yard.

A zombie popped up from behind the shrubs like a puppet in a show, its mouth open wide, the tongue hanging out as drool slid down its chin. There was no solid flesh on its face, only bits and pieces, and the grinning skull glared at Mary, taking her completely off guard. Maggots squirmed in the hollow nasal cavity and a fat worm hung out of one ear canal.

Mary stood immobile, staring at the hideous face, and as the zombie leaned forward to bite her, she jumped back, her feet shuffling side by side.

She was so focused on the zombie before her that she didn't see where she was going, and she backed up and tripped over an old bicycle lying in the gutter. As she fell, her arms went out to both sides to catch her. She fell right onto the bike and as she did, she let out a blood-curdling scream as the jutting, rusted kickstand impaled her right thigh.

Flashes of light filled her vision and she thought back to when shed been shot with her own gun more than a year ago. This pain seemed much worse as the kickstand was still in her thigh, and when she tried to move, the wound opened more.

The zombie was crashing through the bushes, falling over itself to reach her. As she cleared her vision, she found herself looking up at the ghoul, its hands already reaching for her.

Luckily, she still held her .38, and as the zombie lunged for her, looking like a male partner about to climb on her for sex, she shot it once in the neck, then adjusted her aim and put one between its eyes.

The body fell to the side and landed next to her, the black hole in its brow dripping a dark ichor. Mary turned away and cried out as she moved her leg.

She was in such a position that she couldn't get off the kickstand and the agony she felt made her want to pass out.

It was as she began to grow faint that she heard voices calling out and footsteps heading her way.

Henry surveyed the pile of debris he'd gathered in the kitchen.

Everything from old sheets to rags found in the garage, were now piled high directly on top of Emily's skeletal frame. Even what remained of the other skeletal corpses had been brought to the pile after Henry used his panga to pick up and place the remains onto Emily's lap.

Some old newspapers found in the living room provided the kindling needed to get the blaze going and keep it burning long after he'd left.

He made sure to lay enough paper across the floor and in the other rooms so the conflagration would continue to grow, and without hesitation, he lit a rolled up newspaper and tossed it onto the pile.

He was confident he'd chosen material from around the house that wasn't fireproof. It caught almost immediately, and he had to take a step back from the heat as he watched the flames grow higher.

He turned and entered the living room where he had made another small pile of debris, including more than one dried husk of a body. Lighting another piece of paper, he dropped it on the kindling and watched it burn.

This was something he should have done the last time he was here, but in the rush to escape the zombies coming through the house, there had been no time.

Fire was cleansing, and as the living room began to burn and the flames jumped to the curtains, he stepped into the main foyer that led to the front door.

Turning to face the kitchen, he nodded at the place where Emily was hidden under the burning debris, smoke already filling the house. "Rest in peace, honey." He'd finally returned to give her a proper burial, even if it was one that consisted of fire.

The fire popped and spit, crackling filling the house, so at first Henry didn't make out the scream of pain from outside. But a second later, he heard gunshots and there was no doubt in his mind that it was Mary's .38.

Spinning on his heels, he pulled his Glock from his hip and raced out of the house, the heat of the funeral pyre warming his back briefly before he was through the door.

"Jesus, it hurts," Mary said, gritting her teeth in pain.

"Don't move," Cindy warned as she leaned down to inspect the wound. The others surrounded Mary, like a herd protecting a wounded member of the pack.

"How bad is it?" Jimmy asked.

Cindy shrugged. "Well, I'm no doctor but it's not good." She looked at Mary, who had tears in her eyes from the pain. "We need to lift you off the bike. It's gonna hurt."

"No shit," Mary replied. "Just do it, damn it. I feel like a shish-kabob." They all knew she was in real pain, as Mary rarely cursed.

Cindy gestured to Sue and Raven. "You two get her shoulders, Jimmy, get her left leg as I hold her right. On the count of three, we pick her straight up and off the kickstand."

Everyone did as they were told, getting into position. Cindy locked gazes with Mary. "You ready for this? It's gonna hurt."

Mary nodded slowly, her brown hair falling across her face. "Do it already," she growled, her teeth clamped tight.

"Okay, one...two...*three*," Cindy said, and on three, the companions raised Mary, the kickstand sliding out of her thigh with a meaty suction. Mary screamed once, then held it in check as she was moved a few feet to the left and placed on the ground. Her breathing was shallow, and sweat beaded on her cold brow. Jimmy went and dragged the zombie she'd shot a few feet away so none of them had to look at it.

Cindy let go of Mary's leg and moved to the wound, clamping her hands over both ends. Blood squirted between her fingers. "Jesus, we need to get a tourniquet on this. I think she might have hit an artery or something."

It was Raven who came to the rescue. She tore off the sleeve of her shirt and handed it to Cindy. With a brief nod of thanks, Cindy gestured to Jimmy with her chin, as she didn't want to let go of Mary's wound. "Jimmy, take that and get over here. I need you to tie it around Mary's leg, just above the wound."

"Okay," Jimmy said, doing what he was told. Cindy looked at Sue and said, "Sue, get me a stick or a tree branch, about a foot long if possible."

"Done," Sue said and began searching the street. It took seconds for her to find something, thanks to the debris covering the road. When she held it up, Cindy had Jimmy take it.

"Now, Jimmy," Cindy said. "Slide the stick between the knot you made on the tourniquet, then you can spin the stick to tighten and loosen it as needed. We can't leave it on too long or it will restrict blood flow to the leg and she could end up losing it."

"Will do," Jimmy said and did as instructed.

As everyone stood around Mary, concern in their eyes, no one was watching the area around them. Thanks to Mary's gunshot, every zombie that had been hidden within nearby homes and structures was now on the hunt, seeking out the source of the report.

Circled around Mary, their backs to the area, no one saw the five zombies slowly shambling up behind them.

And by the looks of it, the group would never see them until it was too late.

It was the smell Jimmy detected first. A fetid smell, one of decay and death. Sickly sweet, it stuck to the back of the mouth, embedded itself into the nasal cavity, where all the blowing and hacking wouldn't get it out.

He was reaching for his shotgun, which he'd placed on the ground, even as the first zombie reached him. As he spun around, his peripheral vision caught the rotting face and he saw its mouth open wide to take a bite out of his cheek, or perhaps it was going for his neck.

In that blink of an eye, he saw he would be too late to prevent it, that after all the battles he'd fought, he was about to be killed because he hadn't bothered to check over his shoulder.

And then the face exploded, the decayed skull shattering into a dozen pieces of dark blood and brain matter. The headless zombie dropped backwards and landed on its butt before toppling over. The body slowed the other four down, as they now had to either go around or step over the corpse.

In that time, Jimmy was on his feet, as was Cindy, their weapons leveled at the four remaining ghouls. It was over in seconds, as the two warriors blasted the zombies apart, taking off arms and legs before finally controlling their shots and hitting heads.

As the bodies dropped to the pavement, ichor dripping out of large holes, Jimmy turned to see Henry racing up to them, his Glock in his hand.

"Nice shot, old man. You saved my ass," Jimmy said as Henry slowed and knelt down by Mary.

"Pay me back whenever you want," Henry replied, the matter forgotten. Saving each other was a common occurrence and was what made them all a tight-knit family. "Mary, what happened?" he asked, touching her face, feeling how cold she was.

Mary smiled wanly and chuckled. Her body was going into shock from the wound. "I dropped my guard and a deader got the drop on me. I'm so sorry, Henry."

"Shhh, it's okay, it's not important." He looked at Cindy, who shrugged.

"It's not good, Henry. She needs medical help fast. I think she hit an artery or major vein." Cindy shook her head. "I don't know. I'm not a doctor."

"Shit," Jimmy said from beside them and all faces looked up to see him peering over their heads and down the street. All eyes went to follow his and their mouths opened in horror at what greeted them.

The street was filling with zombies, dozens of them, a hundred if not more. They spilled out of every house, garage and backyard.

Henry surveyed the scene and turned to the others. "We need to get out of here. There's too many to fight." He bent down and picked up Mary, cringing when she moaned. "Sorry, honey," he whispered. "Everyone back to the car—hurry." But when they turned to begin the race to their vehicle, Henry saw it was already too late. The ghouls had cut off their path back to the car; there was no way to reach it.

Jimmy fired a shot behind them and all eyes went to see more zombies filling the street. They were now coming from all directions, the center of the circle where the companions stood.

Cindy fired a few rounds, taking down a few more bodies. Headshots all, the ghouls dropped heavily to remain limp. The others in line simply stepped over their fallen brethren, their eyes only for the prey before them.

"This doesn't look good," Cindy said as she fired three more rounds. She kept her fear in check, using the weapon on semi-auto, and used controlled bursts each time she fired.

Instinct born of fear wanted her to just open up and spray the mob of undead with hot lead, but she knew that would be wasteful and counterproductive. Slow, precise shots were the way to go.

"We're trapped," Sue said. "Henry, what do we do?"

"Stay calm, Sue, we need to focus. There's always a way out," he said. He shifted Mary in his arms and wished he could pull his Glock, but he only had two hands and holding Mary was more important. Her eyes were partially closed and he believed she had fainted.

Still, one thing at a time. The first was to escape the deathtrap they found themselves in. "Look for a hole in their ranks; anything will do. We need to punch through and make a run for it."

The companions did as he said, now focusing on finding a weak link in the attacking horde.

"There, I think I see one," Raven said and pointed behind them. Henry spun around, and sure enough, there was a small gap in the ranks of approaching bodies.

"There, widen that hole," Henry ordered. "Shoot any of them near it as we run for it. Jimmy and Cindy, you take point, Sue and Raven follow behind me. Ready? Move out!"

He began running, Mary bouncing in his arms, with Cindy and Jimmy in the lead. As they approached the zombies, they shot each one to widen the hole, then sped through it, spraying lead indiscriminately on both sides to keep the ghouls at bay.

Henry ran through the gap, pale hands swiping at him. One hand grabbed Mary's leg and he kicked out, sending the ghoul flying away to fall into its brethren. Sue had her .22 out and she shot three zombies in the head, the small caliber rounds bouncing within the skulls before exiting, leaving a small exit wound but still taking down the attacker.

Raven slashed out, kicking and punching.

Then they were free of the crowd and on the other side. The zombies began turning around, realizing their prey was now behind them, while the horde from the opposite side of the street joined the ranks on the opposing side. The crowd became one massive horde, some knocking each other over as they turned to follow the companions.

It would have been comical if the situation wasn't so dire. Zombies weren't smart in the best of times and over a hundred on one street, each one following the one before it, caused for some humorous mishaps before they began moving off after the group of fleeing humans.

More than one ghoul was pushed to the ground where its brethren would step over it, crushing it, killing it and then leaving the flattened corpse to rot in the sun.

But soon, they were all facing the correct direction and were pursuing the group of six en masse.

When the companions had a little distance from the following horde, Jimmy slowed so Henry could catch up to him. "What next?"

"We keep running," Henry said and did just that, while behind him and the others, a wall of walking dead gave chase.

A half hour later, Henry paused to lean against a car. The vehicle was covered in filth, half the windows smashed, two of its tires flat from sitting for years. He propped his arms on the hood, resting with Mary between them.

The others stopped as well, though no one was happy about it.

A hundred feet away and closing, the undead horde still followed.

"Come on, Henry, we need to keep moving," Jimmy said quickly, his eyes locked on the pursuing dead.

"Don't you think I know that? Shit, Jimmy, you carry Mary for a while and we'll see how fast *you* can run."

In Henry's arms, Mary was unconscious, her right leg covered in blood that still seeped from the wound, despite the tourniquet.

"Stop fighting, both of you," Cindy said. "All we can do is keep moving and hope we find a car or something." She stepped closer to Henry. "Are you okay? Jimmy may be a jerk but he has a point. How long can you keep this up?"

Henry set his jaw, his eyes closing halfway. "As long as I have to." He stood up, shifted Mary to get her in a better position, and began jogging. The others looked at one another and took off after him.

The chase was on again with them as the prey.

"You guys should go on ahead, don't wait for me," Henry panted as he jogged down the middle of the street. Two miles were behind him since the chase began.

"Screw that," Jimmy said and waved Cindy over to him. "Give her to me and Cindy, we can carry her for a while."

"You sure?" Henry's face was flushed red, his shirt soaked in sweat, but the relief on his face was evident.

"Yeah, we got her." Jimmy took Mary from him and Cindy got on his other side, and with Mary in their arms like a swing, they began to fast-walk. Henry's arms felt like lead weights; he could barely move them. Sue stepped up and hugged him as they started moving again. She wanted to take his pain, his exhaustion, away but knew she couldn't.

Behind the group, the dead still followed, never slowing, never needing to rest.

Flexing his right hand and fingers, Henry waited until he had enough feeling to draw his Glock, then he stopped running, turned, and fired off three shots at the lead zombies.

Heads snapped back and the bodies toppled to the ground, and were immediately enveloped as the rest of the horde walked over them, the fallen bodies irrelevant in their eyes.

As he jogged, Henry wracked his mind with a solution to their problem. His eyes went to the houses on either side, but he knew there was no respite there.

There were so many zombies behind them that the second the companions chose to hole up in a house, they would be sur-rounded. And there was no time to barricade every window and door. They would be overwhelmed within minutes of entering the abode.

His eyes went to the stalled cars and trucks on either side of him, some in the middle of the street. There was nothing he could use, every single vehicle having been stripped of useable parts long ago.

Though they had seen no other signs of survivors, their forag-ing skills were apparent to anyone who knew what to look for.

Shaking his arms to get the blood flowing some more, he concentrated on jogging, his eyes on Jimmy and Cindy. He could see they were already slowing down, the weight of Mary too much for them.

He knew in ten minutes or less he would have to take her back, for though he was only a man with the strength of one, he would carry Mary until all he could do was crawl, and then he would still keep going.

Until he simply couldn't move another inch.

Henry was in the middle of the group as he shifted Mary in his arms for the hundredth time. God she was heavy, or so it seemed to him. It had been two hours since they had begun running for their lives.

The wind had shifted and the miasma of death floated over them all. Sue had her nose covered with her shirt and Raven had taken a peace of cloth and wrapped it around her lower face. Jimmy and Cindy ignored the smell, though Henry could see the distaste on both of their faces.

He knew where he was, though he hadn't visited the neighborhood often when he'd lived in the area. It was filled with massive homes and large lawns, most having tall fences either of wrought iron or molded plastic.

Fifteen feet ahead, Sue and Raven were in the lead, with Jimmy and Cindy following behind Henry to watch his back.

There was an intersection that doglegged to the right coming up and Henry watched Sue and Raven reach it. Then they abruptly stopped.

"Why are you guys stopping?" Henry called as he sucked in air. "Keep going."

They didn't reply, only stared at something Henry couldn't see yet. He imagined what they had discovered. Was it another horde of zombies? Maybe a large tribe of cannibals? Wild dogs, a pack of twenty? The list went on and on in the world of lawlessness and death he now lived in.

When he reached the others, he opened his mouth to chastise them for stopping but then he slowed as well, seeing what had halted them.

Fifty feet away, blocking the entire street, was a tall, twelve foot high fence made of molded plastic, white for the most part but there were other colors such as tan and dark brown mixed in; the last color was supposed to resemble cherry wood. The fence was really two fences, one placed on the other, then jury-rigged together with planks of wood.

It blocked the entire street and then went left and right into the adjoining yards on either side.

But the worst part was the walking dead—about two dozen of them—that were clamoring at the fence, slapping it with their fists. In these places, the once pristine white was covered in pus and gore, as if a mad painter had tried to add his artistic inspiration to the fence's white canvas.

Jimmy looked before him and then behind, at the approaching horde that was now getting closer with each second. "Shit, Henry, we can't get over that. This is so fucked."

"We could shoot the deaders at the fence," Cindy suggested. "There's not as many as behind us."

"Then what?" Henry asked. "Even if we put them all down, we still have to scale the fence, and I'm all out of climbing gear."

Sue moved closer to Henry. "We need to decide quickly, they're getting closer."

"We fight," Raven said, flexing her arms in preparation for the coming battle.

Henry shook his head. "Not this time, Raven, there's simply too many of them. We'll be overrun."

"Then what do we do?" Cindy asked, her rifle gripped tightly in her hands. Her knuckles shone white, she was gripping the weapon so hard in frustration.

Henry shook his head. "I don't know."

The trailing horde was so close that individual traits could now be seen of the first ones in line. A postal worker, still with a bloody mail bag on his shoulder, a housewife in curlers and bathrobe, half her stomach missing.

There was a cook to a fast food restaurant, the large M on his shirt apparent to anyone who saw it. A cable service technician, his tool belt hanging off his hip, and a policeman, rounded out the melting pot of American trades. There were dozens more behind them, all hungry and eager to feed.

Henry shifted Mary over his shoulder in a fireman's carry so he could draw his Glock, feeling slightly better with the weapon in his hand. She moaned softly, but was unconscious.

Blood covered Henry's clothes from where it had seeped from Mary's wound. It was sticky and cold after cooling. He glanced at Mary, her face hidden by her hanging hair and realized the promise he had once made to always protect her was about to be reneged on.

They were trapped. Someone had built a barricade across the town and there was no way to scale it. On top of that, the zombies at the fence had now begun turning to face the companions, seeing prey right before them.

Henry knew this wasn't good. Though he had managed to get himself and his friends out of worse scrapes in the past, he didn't see a way to escape the trap they had seemingly stumbled into.

There was simply no way to survive.

With casual aim, he raised the Glock and fired at one of the zombies, and the fast food cook went down with a bullet in the right eye socket. Blood and brain matter mixed with skull fragments exploded out of the rotting skull to bathe the zombies behind it.

None seemed to mind, well, except for one ghoul that got a piece of skull fragment in its left eye. The bone piece was like grenade shrapnel, and the eye was punctured like an egg. As a pus-like ooze slid down the zombie's cheek, it stumbled onward, its remaining eye leading the way.

The others looked at Henry, not understanding why he'd shot one lone zombie.

He turned to face the others. "Look, guys, I don't see a way out of this. There's nowhere to go. We're trapped. But if we're going down, we'll take as many of them with us as we can. I say we take out the smaller group by the fence, then put our backs against it and hold off till our ammo runs out. Then we use blades and hands till…well, you know."

He saw the faces of each of his friends fill with emotion as they took on the weight of what he'd said. But they were all warriors, even Sue, who had slowly become tougher since joining the companions, and becoming something more to Henry.

"We're with you, old man," Jimmy said, holding his shotgun level as he began double checking it.

"Okay, then, let's do this and send these bastards back to Hell!"

With weapons ready, the battle hardened friends turned together and faced the two dozen zombies coming for them, leveled their guns, and with a battle cry from Henry, they ran at the ghouls, firing as they went.

The next minute and half went by in a blur for Henry and his friends. Gunshot after gunshot found its mark, as zombie after zombie was shot and killed. Heads were blown off, eyes imploded as rounds found their targets, and limbs were taken off to leave jagged stumps that leaked ichor.

When the last zombie was taken down, the companions found themselves with their backs against the fence, no escape in sight.

Breathing heavily, they stood fast and began firing at the oncoming horde that had been chasing them for miles, as all around them two dozen corpses steamed in the sun.

For the next ten minutes they held the line, taking down the closest zombies. As the ghouls fell, a wall began to build, one of dead bodies. This slowed the rest of the undead, and made it even easier for the companions to kill them.

But no matter how determined Henry and the others were to survive, their stock of ammunition was finite.

Sue was the first to run out, her small .22 clicking dry. Jimmy was next, his shotgun cycling on an empty chamber. He cursed and drew his Bowie hunting knife, the eight inches of steel glistening in the sun.

Cindy had kept calm and had used her M-16 on single fire, but even she soon found herself out of bullets and no spare clips.

Raven used Mary's .38, the girl's distaste for firearms overcome given the dire circumstances. That is until her firing pin landed on an empty chamber.

Henry was last, with half a clip remaining. He turned to look down at an unconscious Mary, her back against the fence, her hair covering her sweat-covered face.

"I'm out!" was the saying for the moment, and Henry cringed each time he heard it.

A zombie in a tattered golf suit, complete with a tiny alligator emblem on its chest, went down with half its head missing as Henry shot the ghoul in the face. Shifting his aim, he took out a woman in an evening gown, the once tan dress now black from dried blood and gore.

Popping the clip, he counted how many bullets he had remaining. Seven total. One for each of them and one left over.

Popping the clip back in, he shot a meter maid in the head, the zombie's hat flying off to land in the midst of the other ghouls.

Six bullets remaining. He was standing a few feet behind the others as they prepared for hand to hand combat. Noble, but futile in the end. It would be a hard death, and worse, it was possible they would return as one of the walking dead.

Better to shoot his friends in the head, to end it quick, before they even knew it was happening. The hardest thing would be when he had to take his own life, to put the gun in his mouth and pull the trigger. When it was time, he had to wonder if he would have the courage, or would he end up trying to fight, though the task would be doomed.

Biting his lip as guilt filled him for what he was about to do, he leveled the Glock at the back of Jimmy's head, wanting to take out his old friend first. He placed his finger on the trigger. He squeezed it just a little, knowing only another ounce of pull would be all it would take to fire the pistol.

* * *

Time seemed to slow down for Henry Watson as he stared at the back of Jimmy Cooper's head. It was like he was someone else, and was merely watching events from the sidelines. He saw Jimmy spinning his shotgun around, prepared to use it as a club in his right hand, while his left hand held his hunting knife.

Beside him, Cindy stood defiant, her rifle held in both hands to be used as a bludgeon. To her right was Raven, in a fighting stance, her arms held out before her in readiness of the final battle. Sue was just turning to look at Henry and he saw the amazed look on her face when she realized what he was about to do.

Behind him on the ground, Mary moaned softly, her voice lost in the cacophony of groans and growls made by the encroaching dead.

It was all so surreal, like a dream, one where he had no control, where he could only stare and watch, helpless to act, helpless to change the inevitable outcome.

In a micro-second before he finished the squeeze on the trigger and sent Jimmy on the last train west, a voice called out from over head, as if God himself was making Himself known.

"Ahoy down there! Need some help?" a booming voice called, amplified by a bullhorn.

Henry lowered the Glock and looked up to the top of the fence, as did his friends. Where before the fence had been empty, there were now ten men all armed to the teeth.

"We'll drop the ramp! Get to it before those walkers reach you or it'll be too late!"

Twenty feet to the companion's left, a giant ramp—similar to what would be found to board a naval vessel—swung out from the top of the fence and was then lowered. A small crane was used to move it. The top part of the ramp was situated at the top of the fence, and as the ramp was lowered, it made a gangway for personnel to enter.

No one paused to look a gift horse in the mouth. Henry slapped Jimmy on the back to get him moving as he turned to pick up Mary. "You heard the man. Let's move!"

From above, the crack of gunshots filled the air as the men on the fence line began shooting the approaching dead.

With each gunshot another zombie went down. As the companions ran, a ghoul in a torn dress, the gaping flap exposing the dead woman's anemic thighs, lunged for Sue. Henry got a brief glimpse of the dead woman's face, and saw how her skin was separating from her bones, baggy in places. Her flesh was like an ill-fitting suit. Ichor draped her inner thighs, as if she was menstruating.

With one of his remaining bullets, Henry shot her in the face. The round hit the woman in the mouth, blowing out her front teeth and sending them out the back of her skull, along with the bullet. Her filthy hair billowed out as the skull exploded, then the body dropped to the ground. Sue never saw any of this, she was too focused on running.

The ramp struck the ground with a rattling of hollow metal and the companions ran onto it one at a time. Henry was last, and he had to struggle at the steep incline. His legs, already strained to the limit, shook as he made each step.

The ramp shook. He glanced over his shoulder to see the first of the zombies had reached it and were climbing onto it. Turning, he focused on moving upward. Mary stirred in his arms and he repositioned her so he could use one of the handrails to support himself.

From behind, the walking dead climbed faster, catching up to Henry and his burden.

The rest of the group had reached the top of the ramp and were now all standing there, waiting for him. They saw the zombies behind him but had no ammunition; they were helpless to assist him.

Henry was halfway up the ramp when the first ghoul reached him.

He felt the hand on his shoulder and the skeletal fingers dig deep into his skin, only his jacket preventing his flesh from being pierced. He stopped walking, turned, and with his right boot, kicked out, hitting the ghoul directly in its stomach. The dead man doubled over and fetid air whooshed out of lungs no longer in use. Henry was ready, and as the ghoul bent over, he used his knee, bringing it straight up and into the dead man's forehead.

The zombie was thrown back into the ones behind it and knocked them over. The ramp became a tumble of arms and limbs as the stopgap prevented any more from passing. A few tried to climb over the pile and were knocked off to tumble to the ground below. Heads were smashed open, limbs snapped in two, as dark ichor stained the asphalt.

Satisfied he had some lead time, Henry spun around, and began making his way up the ramp again. "Hold on, Mary, we're almost there," he panted to her unconscious form. As if she heard him, she moaned softly.

When Henry reached the top of the ramp, his friends were waiting with open arms. Cindy and Jimmy took Mary from him and laid her down gently on the catwalk they were on.

As Henry stepped off the ramp, he turned to see the zombies slowly regaining their feet, a few crawling out of the pile to then begin the trek up the ramp. For some reason, none of the men on the catwalk were shooting at the zombies on the ramp and Henry found this odd.

A man walked up to Henry and crossed his arms as he surveyed the bodies on the ramp. He looked to be in his fifties with graying hair cut close to his scalp. A military man was Henry's guess, the instant he laid eyes on the man.

Not that Henry needed help in this assessment. The man wore a navy blue shirt, the breast covered in medals and colorful pins. It was the kind of medals and pins one would see on a colonel in the army when wearing his dress uniform.

Wearing the ornaments now, in the middle of a zombie attack, seemed rather pompous to Henry, especially when it was added to the man's denim jeans and tan work boots. A side arm rode the man's hip and a small hunting knife was on the other, though the blade looked more ornamental than for actual use.

All this Henry took in at a glance, his mind making conclusions to someone he had just met.

"What are you going to do about them?" Henry asked the man.

"You will address me as either 'Sir,' or 'The General,' " the man said flatly in a monotone voice. "And as for the walkers…watch and learn." He turned and waved his right hand in the air. The crane operator nodded in reply and Henry watched as the ramp was lifted into the air, then tipped on its side.

Like a dog shaking off fleas, the zombies were thrown from the ramp to tumble to the ground below. Bodies full of decomposing gas exploded on impact, splattering the area with gore and viscera. When the ramp was clear of bodies, it was swung back over and placed gently on the ground inside the perimeter.

"See?" the General said. "No need to waste bullets or risk any of my men."

Henry had to agree it was efficient. "Not bad," he said, then turned to look the man in the eye. "Look, my friend has been cut bad, she needs medical attention immediately. Can you help?"

The General seemed to weigh Henry's request. Four men, two on each side of the companions, each held their rifles trained on the strangers.

Henry didn't think the General meant him or his group any harm. If he'd wanted them dead, all he could have done was just leave them to the zombies below.

Still, if the man proved a threat, well, it wouldn't be the first time they had been saved only to find themselves involved in something more sinister.

A full minute passed in silence, well, other than the moans of the dead below at the fence and the few gunshots sounding every few seconds.

It seemed the General's men had restraint when it came to the zombies. Finally, the man nodded and pointed to two guards a few feet away. "Take the woman to Doc Connors, and then set our new arrivals up in one of the homes not in use."

"Yes, sir," the guard said and gestured for the companions to get moving. Henry paused for a moment and the General smiled, only the gesture was far from friendly. "Go, my friend, you're safe here. The walkers can't get in here. We'll talk after you've rested."

"That sounds fine," Henry said. "And thank you for coming to our aid. I thought this was it for us." He didn't mention how the man had waited far too long before showing his presence.

"Glad to be of assistance. We can always use some more able-bodied personnel here."

"Oh, uhm, thanks, General, but we won't be staying. Once Mary's patched up we can settle on some kind of payment, then we'll be leaving."

The General's face didn't waver but Henry spotted the flicker in the man's eyes of displeasure. "Well, we can discuss that all later after we've been properly introduced and you've rested from your ordeal. Now go, my men and I have to take care of this crowd of walkers. This fence isn't as strong as I'd like it to be."

Henry nodded and walked way, climbing down the scaffolding where the rest of his group was already waiting. The guard led the way and they followed.

Cindy and Jimmy were still carrying Mary, and Henry didn't see a reason to take her back. His arms were killing him and he felt a hundred pounds lighter now that his burden was taken from him.

As they walked, Sue was by his side, Raven a few feet behind. He reached a hand out and slowed her slightly so the others were a few feet before them and out of earshot. Raven saw they wanted privacy and walked past them with a slight glance.

"Listen, Sue, about earlier, when I thought we were about to die horribly. I believed it was the only way out, to…"

She shook her head, her hair caressing her face. "Henry, it's all right. I understand. You don't have to say anything."

"I know, it's just…if you said anything to the others… I don't know if they would understand…" He trailed off.

She smiled. "Well, I understand why you were about to do it and that's all that matters. Your secret is safe with me. I'm just glad you didn't have to do it." She leaned forward and kissed him. He closed his eyes and relished her taste, her soft lips, her warm breath. He was sad when she pulled away.

"Yeah," he replied. "Me too. It really would have put a crimp in our day."

Like many barricaded towns and encampments before the one he was now in, Henry saw the same things. Drawn faces, many covered in dirt and grime, children who hid behind their mother's legs as the strangers passed them by.

None of this was new to Henry or his group of travelers.

They were always the outsiders, the people from beyond the gates, the strangers who were somehow surviving in a world filled with the walking dead.

The group's escort led them deeper into the neighborhood and Cindy began asking the man questions. When the guard looked at her and Cindy smiled, it was all that was needed to pry the information from him. Jimmy hated another man looking at her like that but he knew information was valuable.

"The General's real name is Michael Walters and he's retired Army. When the tainted rains first came and the dead began to walk because of it, he was the one who rallied everyone in a three block radius and got them to build the fence. He was the first to figure out what was happening and deal with it. The fence was taken from nearby front and backyards within the perimeter and it surrounds the whole complex." He waved his arms, gesturing to all around them. "If it wasn't for his quick thinking, hell, none of us would still be alive. We all owe him big time."

"Is that why you let him play war hero?" Jimmy asked.

The guard shrugged. "Hey, the General knows his shit. If he wants to wear a bunch of medals, who am I to judge. Hell, who are you?"

"General Patton he's not," Henry said with a smirk.

The guard stopped walking and looked Henry square in the face. "Don't let the General or any of his trusted men hear you say that."

"Why not?" Jimmy asked.

"Because you'll wind up swinging from a pole over the walkers, that's what. He runs a tight ship and allows no disobedience. No one complains 'cause he keeps this place running. Keeps order, too."

"Where's this Doc Connors located?" Henry asked, impatient to get Mary medical help. He was growing bored with talking about the General. He'd seen men like him dozens of times since the dead began to walk. Men who had small lives or felt forgotten, such as a retired General. Now they made sure they were needed again, and if not, they maneuvered themselves into positions of power. Of course, once in that seat of power, they had to hold it with an iron fist or risk losing it.

"We're almost there," the guard said. "He's on the next block."

"Shit," Jimmy moaned as he carried Mary. "It would have been nice if we had driven there."

The guards shook his head. "We don't have any running vehicles, all the gas dried up over six months ago."

"No shit?" Jimmy said. "Why didn't you go out and see what you could salvage from wrecked and abandoned cars?"

"The General said it wasn't worth the risk," the man said.

Henry saw the guard was around twenty or so and knew that was why he didn't protest the lack of fuel. He was too young to voice his opinion if he disagreed. It was the same reason why the military drafted men as young as eighteen during wars. The men were too young to have a voice yet and were easy to manipulate.

"Do you go outside often?" Henry asked.

"No, not really," the man said. "There have been a few salvage missions over the past two years but we haven't gone out recently. Besides, we have all we need in here. We grow our own food, have a few wells dug for water, and there are enough supplies like candles and stuff to last for years, thanks to all the empty homes and a department store we raided way back when it all began. We took everything that wasn't nailed down and stored it in a couple of empty houses on the edge of the perimeter. We did the same to a supermarket about five miles from here."

"But surely you'll run out of things eventually," Sue said. "Candles burn down and water wells dry up sometimes, and canned food won't last forever."

"The General says to take one day at a time, ma'am," the man said, then pointed to a small house at the corner of the street. "That's Doc Connors' place." The two-way radio crackled on the guard's hip and he withdrew it and placed it to his ear.

"Tyler here, sir,"

"Get back over here now, son, we need more help clearing these damn walkers away," the General's voice crackled.

"Yes, sir, I'm on my way." Tyler looked at Henry, sensing he was the one in charge of the small group. "You can go on without me. Just tell Doc the General sent you." Before Henry could respond, the man sprinted away.

He was gone in seconds.

"You heard him, let's go. Mary needs to be looked at fast," Henry said.

Jimmy and Cindy picked up their pace as they reached and then entered the small house.

Henry was first in and he held the door for Jimmy and Cindy as they carried Mary inside.

"Hello? We need some help here!" Henry called out. The foyer was sparse and led straight into another room. The aroma of bleach and antiseptic floated in the air, reminding Henry of a time when things were normal, before the dead began to walk. It seemed like a lifetime ago, as if it all had been lived by someone else.

"What the hell? Damn it, where is everyone?" Henry yelled again. Sue and Raven entered the home, and as Sue went to Henry, Raven jogged off deeper into the home.

A few seconds later, she retuned, leading a man in a wool sweater and black slacks. A pair of loafers adorned his feet, and on the top of his graying scalp rode a pair of wire-rimmed glasses, each side connected with a thin chain so he could hang them from his neck if he chose. Henry saw a fishing magazine in his hand.

"Who are you people?" the man asked, his eyes moving to each face in the group. But when his gaze rested on Mary in the arms of Jimmy and Cindy, it was all he needed to know. "Here, bring her back here," he said and rushed off. No one needed to be told to follow, and with Henry in the lead, the companions moved deeper into the house.

Down a short hallway there were doors, each with a number on it. Henry knew then that this man was a general practitioner who had run his practice from inside the home. He'd seen many doctors' offices that were set up in houses, and always assumed it was so the patient felt more relaxed compared to having to go to a standard building with steel and cement and other offices inside as well. As he moved down the hallway, and looked at the flower and ocean paintings on the wall, he had to admit that the effect was working, if only slightly.

Doc Connors—for who else could the man be?—turned into a room with the door already open. "Here, here, put her on the table," he said and went to a counter and began donning rubber gloves. Other than the lack of electricity, everything felt normal.

Jimmy took Mary from Cindy and picked her up completely, then placed her on the table. Henry watched this from behind, impressed with Jimmy's strength. Only two years ago, Jimmy had been a skinny kid with long hair and a wise mouth.

Though he still had a wise crack for every occasion, his physique had filled out and his skin was now dark brown from exposure to the sun. He was basically a reflection of Henry, only younger.

Henry glanced down at his hands, seeing the scars on his arms, the calluses on his fingers. It had been a hard road these past two years, but he had traveled it willingly with his new friends.

He was pulled from his reverie as Doc Connors began talking more to himself than the group. "Laceration to the right thigh, deep, torn ligaments by the look of it." Mary groaned softly but the doctor ignored her; he was all business and the patient was a living being only by default. "Looks like a vein was nicked. Lucky, if it had been an artery she would be dead by now." He looked up. "How did this happen?" he asked the room.

"She fell down onto a bicycle kickstand," Jimmy said, stepping closer. He reached down and touched Mary's arm. "A deader tried to make her lunch and she tripped."

Doc Connors looked confused for a moment. "A deader? What's a..." Then it snapped into place and he understood. "Ah, you mean a walker. Yes, of course, what else would it be?" He went to the counter and grabbed a tray of instruments. He quickly returned to Mary's side and placed them at the foot of the table. Then he went and took a dark brown bottle of something no one knew the contents of out of a cabinet.

"Ether," he said, holding up a small cloth as he poured some into the material. "We don't want her waking up and I'm afraid I don't have an anesthesiologist."

"You need to knock her out?" Cindy asked.

"Yes, dear, most definitely," Doc Connors said. "I need to operate on her. I need to get in there and stitch that vein up." He looked at Sue. "You, I need you to stay and assist me."

"Me, Why?" Sue asked.

"No reason," the doctor replied. "I don't have a nurse and I need a set of hands. I decided to pick you."

Sue looked at Henry who nodded. "Do it, Sue, whatever it takes to help Mary."

"Of course, Henry, that's not why I asked," she said.

"Excellent, then let's get started," Doc Connors said. He began shooing the others out of the cramped room. "Go wait outside. I'll call you when I'm done, now go, shoo, shoo. Let me work in peace."

The companions shuffled out of the room and Henry heard Doc Connors telling Sue to don rubber gloves, then the door was kicked closed and his voice was muffled to the point of being indecipherable.

They stood in the hallway, looking at one another. Henry gestured to the front of the house. "Come on, let's get some air."

"I hope Mary's gonna be all right," Jimmy said, the others nodding in agreement.

"Yeah, me too," Henry added.

They filed outside and stood around, making small talk, but then simply remaining silent. Everyone was concerned for Mary. A few people walked by, staring at the strangers, but no one stopped to say hello.

After ten minutes had passed without anyone speaking, Henry turned so that each of them was looking at him. "Okay, people, we're not doing ourselves any good standing around here. We need to keep busy."

"What do you have in mind, old man?" Jimmy asked.

"We need to resupply for one thing, so let's get going on it," Henry said and pointed at Jimmy. "You and Cindy go and see how this place is set for ammo, and I'm gonna go back to that wall and see how these people handle the deaders." He pointed a finger at Raven. "You stay here with Sue and Mary. If anything comes up we need to know, come find the rest of us."

"Got it," Raven said simply.

"Good, we'll all meet back here in half an hour." Henry turned to walk away and then stopped, turning back to Jimmy and Cindy. "And you guys find us a place to wash up and eat."

"Will do, old man, and don't break a hip while we're all separated," Jimmy quipped with his patented wiseass grin.

Henry was going to reply back but stopped himself. This was why Jimmy called him that, to get a rise out of him. Instead of speaking, he waved with a polite smile and walked off.

"Huh, how 'bout that," Jimmy said under his breath as Henry walked away without so much as telling him to shut up.

Cindy chuckled. "Looks like you're losing your edge, lover," she said while patting him on the shoulder. "Come on, let's go find someplace to eat. I'm starving and there's nothing we can do for Mary out here anyway."

"Yeah, fine, let's go." He nodded to Raven, who was already leaning against the house with her eyes half closed. She was like a cat waiting to spring at an unsuspecting mouse. She had already decided to wait another ten minutes and then was going to go back inside and check on Mary's status.

Henry walked back through the small complex, his eyes taking in everything he could. He only saw a few men on patrol, and each of them had made eye contact and then moved on. He found it odd that neither the General nor his guards minded that he or his team still carried their weapons. In other barricaded towns he and his group had come across, the first thing to be removed from the companions were their firearms.

Henry wondered if the General knew that they were out of ammunition other than Henry's Glock and that was the reason he had let the group keep their weapons. Either that, or the man was one of two things: trusting or confident that Henry and company couldn't do anything to hurt him within the walls.

He had to admit, he was impressed with what he saw. Homes were clean, as were the streets, people seemed friendly enough, and the wall was a secure deterrent from the living dead. It seemed every place he came across looked good on the outside but deep underneath, there was something rotten, like an apple with a decayed core, yet the outer skin looked pristine.

Perhaps this would be the one place that everything would be as it looks, just a bunch of people gathered together for a common good, all trying to survive in a world where the dead walked and wanted to feast on the living.

He smelled that he was getting close before he rounded a corner and saw the wall and scaffolding before him. He'd needed to ask for directions only once, then all he had to do was simply follow the sounds of moaning, yelling of guards, and the odor of human decay.

It was an odor a person never forgot, a putrefying stench that hit the owner's senses like a wall, a miasma of rot that seemed to slide into the nasal cavity and take root. Most men simply puked as soon as they walked into the odor, but some, like Henry, had learned to ignore it, to force his gut from rebelling against the undeniable redolence of festering human meat.

When he was twenty feet from the wall, he had a clear view of the activity above it. Men were moving back and forth, and dropping what appeared to be concrete blocks once use for building foundations. The blocks had a rope tied to them so each man dropping his could retrieve it.

Henry climbed up the scaffold, ignoring the odd looks of the guards, who wondered what he thought he was doing.

The General saw him and walked over.

"Mary's in good hands so I thought I'd come back and see if I could lend a hand," Henry said.

The General shrugged, his medals jangling from the gesture. "Appreciate the sentient but as you can see, my men have things well in hand." He turned and pointed at a guard who was just pulling up his makeshift bludgeon. "Kevin, move down a few feet and clean up that group of walkers."

"Yes sir," Kevin replied and shifted to where the General wanted him. He began dropping the cement block again.

Henry watched the block tumble downward where the corner of it connected with the face of a zombie. The ghoul had been looking up at the time of impact and its jawbone was dislodged, driving the sharp spear of bone directly into its brain.

The sudden alteration of the zombie's features made the thing look like an old man that had lost all its teeth. Then the rest of the block connected with the pale face and was pushed in, entirely demolishing the visage into nothing but red mush.

Kevin began pulling on the rope like a sailor pulling in a small anchor. The gore-covered block banged against the fence and scraped its facade as it was slowly brought up.

Henry watched the exact same tableaux all down the fence. Guards picked a target and let fly, the weight of the block more than enough to cave in a head or snap a neck. Henry was impressed. This was a clever way to take out countless zombies without ever firing a shot.

He was about to comment on this when the man called Kevin let out a scared yelp. Henry and the General both turned as one to see Kevin going over the side of the fence.

Henry's eyes looked down where two zombies had managed to grab the rope the cement block was attached to and had yanked on it, pulling Kevin into their midst.

Kevin's arms flapped by his side as he went over, as if he could do this fast enough and mange to simply fly over the sea of dead and land back on the wall.

But of course, that wasn't what happened. The man plummeted straight down, his eyes wide in terror, his tongue hanging out of his mouth like a cartoon character.

He didn't die when he landed on top of the sea of bodies. Henry thought the scene reminded him of a mosh pit, where the singer would jump off the stage and into the welcome arms of the waiting crowd.

There was no doubt about it that Kevin was welcomed with open arms...and teeth, and hands.

The zombies began attacking him immediately, sharp fingernails tearing at his clothes and the flesh beneath. Kevin lost an ear when an old woman sank her dentures into his earlobe and pulled, the skin stretching like pink taffy.

Another two dove into his abdomen, clawing at the soft flesh and soon making a hole where intestines were pulled out like garland from a Christmas storage box. Kevin's screams quickly turned to shrieks of agony as he was torn apart inch by inch.

It was as he screamed, his mouth open wide, that a zombie reached in and grabbed his tongue, pulling it out as if it was an eel hiding in its cave. Teeth sank into the flailing muscle and blood squirted out between the two faces. Henry thought it looked like the zombie was kissing the man and he was right, for the kiss of death had never been so aptly named.

Henry couldn't stand to see another human being suffering for no reason, and he was reaching for his Glock to put Kevin out of his misery when he saw the man's head explode in a glorious spray of bone and brain matter. The bullet had been so powerful it not only destroyed Kevin's head but the zombie that had been eating his tongue.

As both bodies slumped to the ground, the zombie was pulled off Kevin's warm and headless corpse and the undead mob began to feed, for the moment not caring that Kevin had no head. If the body was warm they still wanted it.

Henry looked to his left to see the General lowering a high-powered sniper rifle. He handed it back to the guard he'd taken it from and nodded, proud of his marksmanship.

"Okay, you boys take care of the rest of these walkers, then send out some men to drag them away from the fence and torch the entire lot."

"Yes, sir," the guard said as he stared down at the feeding frenzy.

"And for God's sakes, tell the men to be careful. That's the second man that's happened to in as many months."

"Yes, sir, I'll take care of it," the guard said.

The General turned and began walking away, but paused as he passed Henry. "When you're done here, come see me in my office. Just ask anyone, they'll direct you." He didn't wait for a reply, but descended the scaffolding and walked away.

Henry watched the man go and wondered if this General wasn't as pompous as he first believed. He walked over to the guard who held the sniper rifle and said, "That was something. It happen often?"

The man shrugged. "A few times. Gotta be careful is all. If they get a grip on the rope, you're supposed to just let go and get another block. Once they're all down it's easy to retrieve any blocks we've lost."

"So then why did that guy not let go?"

The man shrugged yet again. "He was stupid."

"That was something else. Your General shot that man without blinking," Henry stated.

The guard chuckled then and Henry found that odd given the circumstances. "What's so funny?"

"What's so funny is that wasn't just a guy on guard duty. That was the General's son-in-law. Now he's gotta tell his daughter what happened."

Henry didn't reply, but instead watched the men on the wall dropping concrete blocks on the zombies' heads. The wet *smack* of stone on flesh was revolting but Henry had seen and heard worse in his travels.

Fat blowflies hovered over the crowd, feeding on the dead flesh, and beetles crawled on the ground from where they'd been knocked out of holes in the walking dead corpses. An entomologist would have had a field day.

He stayed for another ten minutes, watching the guards kill the zombies, then grew bored. More than half had been downed when he decided it was time to get back to Mary and the others. He was worried and wanted to know what news there was on her condition.

Saying goodbye to a few of the men, who politely nodded in his direction, Henry climbed down and made his way back to the doctor's home.

"Well, I've cleaned and stitched up the wound and I managed to cauterize the vein that was nicked, but she needs blood and antibiotics desperately," Doc Connors said. He, Henry and the others were standing in the main room of his house. "But I'm afraid I don't have any of either."

Jimmy shook his head in consternation. "What do you mean you don't have any antibiotics? You're a doctor, aren't you?"

"Of course I am, son, but I ran out of the stuff months ago. I've been prescribing aspirin for infections, for God's sake."

"I'm typo O-neg," Sue interjected. "I can donate all the blood you need if it'll help Mary. I'm sorry, I should have told you that before."

Doc Connors nodded and looked relieved. "Ah yes, and I should have asked you all! But that's excellent, it will be perfect."

"But don't you need to know Mary's type, too?" Cindy asked.

Doc Connors shook his head. "No, dear, not at all. O-neg is what we call a universal donor. She's compatible with anyone, which makes her type so rare."

"She is a rare one, that's for sure," Henry said and gave Sue a hug.

"Okay, let's begin at once. Then we can discuss the antibiotics situation," Doc Connors said. He led Sue to Mary's room and rushed the following others off with the exception of Cindy, who would assist in any way she could. Doc Connors explained how an extra set of hands was always welcome.

Henry, Raven and Jimmy waited in the main room for almost an hour before Cindy and Doc Connors returned. Sue was resting in the room with Mary after giving the limit of blood she could handle without going into shock herself.

"How is she, Doc?" Henry asked.

"Slightly better," the man replied. "The transfusion will definitely help, but she's running a fever and her white cells are elevated. She needs antibiotics or else she'll die."

"Then get her some," Henry said flatly.

"That's just it," Doc Connors said. "There's no place that might even have antibiotics other than the hospital in the next town over. I heard they were hit hard when the epidemic first hit and the contaminated rain fell, but it's possible there might be some in one of their storerooms. If you're lucky."

"But no guarantees," Jimmy added. "Shit, it might all be for nothing."

"Better a slim chance than nothing at all," Henry said. "I'll head out in an hour."

"But you can't," Doc Connors said. "It's different out there. There are blockades everywhere and massive clumps of walkers. You could turn a corner and find that there's nowhere to go, and when you try to retreat, you'll find yourself cut off."

"Well, it's not like I have a choice, Doc," Henry said.

"I know that, believe me I do. What I mean is you need a guide, someone who knows the area and how it's changed."

Jimmy stepped so close to the doctor that he could smell his breath. He detected the odor of mint leaves. "And I bet you know someone, don't you?"

"Why, yes, as a matter of fact, I do. For a price he'll go with you and take you through the easiest route."

"A price huh? How much?" Henry asked, then shook his head. With a wave of his hand he said, "Never mind, it doesn't matter. Whatever it is I'll pay it if it will save Mary's life. Set it up, and tell him we leave immediately."

Doc Connors looked pleased. "Good, I'll get right on it. But I warn you, it won't be cheap."

"Just do it," Henry said through gritted teeth. He knew he was being played by what he'd been told. Connors would wait for someone to come in and need help, then the man would strong-arm them for payment if they wanted the patient treated. It was a perfect crime, as there were no other options for the person or persons being blackmailed.

But if it would save Mary then he was all in. When she was on the road to recovery, well, then he and Connors would have another talk.

Connors left the room and a second later a back door opened and closed.

"I'm coming, too," Jimmy said.

Henry shook his head. "No, Jimmy, you stay here and keep an eye on the others. We don't know this place and if anything goes south I want as many of our people together as possible. Besides, if it's just me and one other guy, we can move quicker than with three."

"But what if you run into deaders?" Jimmy asked. "You'll need the extra firepower."

"True, but this isn't a search and destroy mission. The goal is to get the meds and get back here. I plan on doing as little shooting as possible."

"Shit, old man, I still don't like it. This guide will be someone you don't know. How can you trust him?"

Henry grinned, showing off his perfect teeth. "I won't trust him, not completely. But before I go with him, both he and Connors will know what will happen if I don't return." He locked gazes with Jimmy. "You get me?"

It took Jimmy a full second to realize what Henry meant, but then he slowly began to smile. "Yeah, I get you, and don't worry; I'll take care of everything on this end."

"*We'll* take care of everything," Cindy said and Raven chimed in also.

An hour later, Henry and his guide—who called himself Skeeter—rode out of the compound by a back way seldom used, both men on two beat-up motorcycles.

Neither bike had a working ignition, but instead had the wire harnesses exposed, and to start the engines you would simply touch and twist two wires together. Henry's bike was an old Kawasaki with missing fenders and no rubber on the foot pegs.

The gas tank was dented on one side and the paint had been scraped off on the other, plus the handlebars were bent so he had to keep the bike handlebars turned at a ten degree angle, though the tire was facing straight on.

Skeeter's motorcycle faired little better than Henry's. It was an old Honda with a torn seat, dented gas tank, and a front fender so dented and banged up it should be removed from the machine altogether; it was amazing the bike ran at all.

Both motorcycles were covered in dirt, dried blood and muck, as well as grease that had been flung off the chains that pulled the bikes along.

The only good thing about both motorcycles was that the mufflers were well maintained and had been packed with sound-dampening material so that they barely made a sound.

The second Henry had met Skeeter, he'd liked him. Skeeter was in his early fifties with long hair that reached past his shoulder blades. He'd told Henry that since the dead began to walk he hadn't cut it and he wouldn't cut it until the world went back to normal. He carried a sawed-off shotgun over his shoulder and a .45 pistol on his hip.

Henry had managed to buy two more clips for his Glock by trading on what he would bring back in medicine. Doc Connors had vouched for him as well. Without the doctor's backing, Henry wouldn't have been able to get the bullets he so desperately needed. In fact, Doc Connors had pretty much financed the entire operation, right down to paying Skeeter for his services.

Henry had a feeling the good doctor had been waiting for someone like Henry to come along, someone he could use to get the meds he needed. Connors hadn't kept it a secret that the meds Henry were retrieving were worth more than gold in the old world.

Henry didn't care what the man did with the meds, as long as he helped Mary. He glanced at his side mirror to see the tall fence fading away. They had used an exit Skeeter assured Henry that the General didn't even know existed.

It had been nothing more than a hole cut in the fence wide enough to driver a motorcycle through, then large hinges had been added. When it was closed, a heavy four by four was propped against it to make sure any wandering zombies couldn't get in. It was simple but was more than secure enough as long as a large crowd of undead didn't arrive, which was doubtful given the remoteness of the entrance/exit.

They drove out of a backyard where the exit was located and onto the street. Even muffled, the bikes made some noise and a few zombies appeared from where they'd been sitting in bushes or on porches, as if they were dogs waiting for their master to return home. They'd be waiting for a long time if that was so.

Skeeter was in the lead and he simply weaved his way around the stumbling walkers. He got playful and swung his right boot out, catching one in the groin and sending it sprawling.

Henry ignored the man's antics, knowing if you screwed around with the walking dead one too many times, sooner or later you'd find yourself dead as well, or worse, joining them as a zombie.

They each had half a tank of gas, and when Henry had asked Skeeter where he'd come by it, the man had simply grinned his yellow teeth at Henry and winked, as if that said it all.

Skeeter took the lead, knowing the best route to take. Henry didn't mind though he also knew the area. Having lived in this part of the state for years, he found it odd to see the familiar places now so changed.

Homes he once admired for their manicured lawns, handsome paint jobs, and vinyl siding on the houses, were now overgrown weed patches, the homes either partially burnt or covered in so many weeds and kudzu that some of the houses could barely be seen. It never stopped reminding him how fast Mother Nature would take back what was hers. Give it another few years and the homes would be lost within so much foliage they would be nothing but shells for the local animal life.

There was a pile-up ahead on the road and Skeeter's engine cycled down as he slowed, then gestured with his right hand for Henry to follow.

Henry did as told, tracing the path Skeeter made as he drove off the road and around the pile-up. Glancing at the wreckage, Henry barely took in the skeletons still sitting in the drivers' seats, the eyeless sockets still gazing out of cracked windshields on a journey they would never finish. One skull had finally lost its jawbone, the lower jaw ending up in the withered body's lap.

Then he was past the wreckage and on the road again.

It didn't take long for them to be out of town and on the main road leading to the next one, where the hospital would hopefully still be waiting for them. Skeeter had disclosed that fires had been popping up due to such a dry season, and for all he knew the hospital was nothing but rubble.

Henry could only pray that wasn't the case.

As the road opened up and left the suburbs behind and became more rural, the zombies became scarcer. Spread out on the road like lonely hitchhikers, it was easy to avoid them, though Skeeter still couldn't help but want to mess with more than one.

Rounding a corner, Henry spotted four zombies in the middle of the road directly on the yellow line. They were all hunched over something, and as he rode closer, he saw the lump was human-shaped, and when he passed by them, he saw a slender hand jutting out and between the hunched-over figures. Though wrinkled with age, there was a wedding ring reflecting the sunlight on the ring finger.

Skeeter didn't bother with these zombies, and in fact gave them a wide path, but there was something about seeing them there—feeding as if they had nothing to fear—that angered Henry.

He slowed and came to a stop fifteen feet after passing them.

Realizing Henry wasn't following him, Skeeter slowed, stopped, and turned around, then parked next to Henry's bike.

"Whats wrong? Why'd you stop?" Skeeter asked as Henry climbed off his motorcycle and reached down for his panga.

"I'll just be a minute," he said coldly, the panga now in his hand. It had been cleaned and it reflected the sunlight like a polished mirror.

As he began to walk over to the four zombies, Skeeter called, "What're you, crazy? Leave 'em be, they ain't hurtin' no one."

Henry smiled slightly, though the gesture didn't reach his eyes. They weren't hurting anyone. Tell that to the lump of human flesh that had been caught off guard and taken down like a deer to a pack of lions. No, these creatures had to go.

An inner voice told him he was being stupid and he remembered many times telling Jimmy that you couldn't kill every zombie in the world, that it would be a foolish pursuit, but sometimes, just sometimes, they *all* didn't have to be killed. Sometimes, just one or two or four was all it would take to keep a man sane for one more day.

As he moved closer, the quartet of dead didn't stir, too focused on their meal to care about anything else. Henry stepped up behind the first one, its back to him, and without hesitation, he swiped his panga in a horizontal motion, taking the head off the shoulders with one heavy blow.

Henry felt the blade slice through bone and muscle and he was ready for it. Only due to the rotting corpse's condition was he able to do this. He used to laugh how he would see a murderer in a hockey mask in a horror film take a head off as if it was connected by paper. No, to sever a head from a body, it would take much more than a single blow.

The walking dead were mostly rotted flesh and so what seemed ridiculous was in fact quite simple. The head spun in the air, the zombie's mouth still chewing the meat it had stuffed into its maw.

The head bounced once and rolled into the gutter of the road, where a groove had been made to direct rainwater. Lying on its left ear, the head continued to chew, unmindful of its head now without a body.

At the destruction of one of its brethren, the other three snapped out of their feeding frenzy and rose as one, now only having eyes for the new prey.

They came at Henry together, and he used the panga swiftly, slicing the arms off one and kicking the second away, where it fell onto its butt in the road.

But the third got by his guard and wrapped its hands around Henry's neck. Not wanting to take a chance, he dropped the panga to the road and reached down for his Glock, withdrew it, and placed the muzzle under the zombie's chin, its face not more than six inches from his own.

One squeeze of the trigger and the top of the ghoul's head exploded upward, a large piece of its scalp spinning in the air before it splattered onto the road. Mixed with the scalp were bits of gray brains and skull fragments.

The ghoul stumbled for a second, then the hands around Henry's neck went slack and it dropped to the ground. Henry looked past the fallen corpse to see the one he'd kicked rising.

He stepped closer and shot it in the head, then put one in the lump of meat on the ground, just in case the poor woman might return. Then he walked back to Skeeter, only pausing to retrieve his fallen panga.

"Now that sure as hell was a waste of time and three bullets," Skeeter said as he revved the throttle to his bike.

"That's your opinion," Henry said simply. He climbed onto his motorcycle, started the engine, and rode off, leaving Skeeter with one hand on the clutch and the other on his lap. Not wanting to be left behind, he drove off, following Henry.

A half mile from the hospital, Skeeter had them pull over and turn off their engines. When Henry questioned the man on the reasoning behind this, Skeeter had said, "The road is choked with abandoned cars and at the end of the street where the hospital is, there's an old military blockade, so we gotta go the rest of the way on foot, as there's no way to reach the place with even a two wheeler. Not to mention it's quieter. When the rains first fell and the dead began to walk, as you can guess, the hospital was overrun with people, both sick and dying. It was a mess, and it wasn't long before anyone still living was slaughtered by the dead that got inside."

"So what's it like now?" Henry had asked. "Hell, it's been years since that happened."

Skeeter had nodded. "Sure enough. Pretty much the bodies should be nothin' but dried husks and the rats and mice probably took care of even that. Should be nothin' but skeletons by now, I imagine."

"But you don't know for sure?"

Skeeter had spit in the dirt and shrugged. "How would I know? No one's been back here since the place fell apart."

"Then why are you here now, with me?" Henry had asked.

"'Cause Doc Connors is payin' me a king's ransom to help you, that's why."

That had been ten minutes ago. Now, the two men were half-way to the hospital and so far it had indeed been quiet. Picking their way around the wreckage, Henry couldn't help but imagine what it must have been like when the rains first fell and people died and returned. Even after all this time, he had no idea that it had all begun with contaminated water, that once consumed it had caused instant death and then reanimation with a hunger for human flesh. Though he'd been smack dab in the middle of the initial uprising, he'd been far too close to it all to see the picture clearly.

Many of the vehicles had dried husks of bodies in them, and as he passed them, he saw men, women and children, only the clothing and the sizes of the bodies allowing him to differentiate between the sexes.

It was as he was walking by a Toyota four door that a face slammed up against the filthy glass and began to slide down it. Though rotted and covered in puss, the skin soft like putty from being trapped within the car for so long, Henry knew immediately it was a child, roughly the age of seven to ten.

There was no hair left, the scalp having slid off the skull from decay, and one eye had melted, leaving a gaping socket. The nose was askew, looking as if it would slip off the face at any moment. The entire visage reminded Henry of someone who had applied far too much makeup and had then gone outside in one hundred degree heat, the makeup now sluicing off the features.

Skeeter saw that Henry had stopped walking and he turned and joined the deadland's warrior. The second he saw the small ghoul in the car, his face wrinkled in disgust. "What now? You gonna kill this one, too?"

Henry shook his head. "I want to, but no, I'll leave it be." He glanced at Skeeter. "Sometimes I forget these things were once people. I think as soon as you do, each of us loses a part of who we were, you know?"

Skeeter shrugged. "I guess so. The way you killed those walkers out on the road a while back, you could have fooled me you thought like that."

"Yeah, well, it's when I see the ones that were once kids that I really think about it." He turned and began walking up the road, thinking back to a time when he was in the park walking by a fountain where kids were playing in the water. That time of happiness had turned into absolute carnage when the kids had turned and fed on their parents right before his eyes. "Come on, enough talking, we need to get the antibiotics and get back."

Skeeter hawked a loogie and wiped his mouth with the back of his sleeve, then slid in a wad of chewing tobacco. "Enough talking? Shit, it's you that keeps slowin' us down."

"I count fifteen, maybe seventeen," Henry said as he peered over the overturned pickup truck a hundred yards from the hospital. It was hard to get a precise count, as the zombies wouldn't stand still, but milled around in circles like a herd of drunks who'd left the bar after last call and were hanging around outside.

"There's more nearby, no doubt," Skeeter said and put some chewing tobacco into the corner of his mouth. He let the tobacco get good and wet and then spit to his left. The ball of dark fluid soared through the air and splattered on the ground four feet away.

Skeeter looked proud, and when he looked to Henry for a pat on the back, he saw the warrior wasn't paying attention, but was studying the undead crowd once more. "We need a diversion. Some way to get those deaders away from there so we can make a run to the hospital," Henry mused.

Skeeter's face took on one of confusion, then he worked it out in his mind. "Deader huh? You don't call them walkers?" The man looked like he wanted to have a chat about it.

Henry turned to look Skeeter in the eye and his jaw went taut. "Who gives a shit what we call them? In case you've forgotten, my friend is back in Doc Connors place in desperate need of medicine. Now, focus on the task at hand or I'll do it without you."

Skeeter held up his hands in surrender, the sleeves of his shirt sliding up to expose his dirty arms. "Hey, whoa there, big guy, it's all good. I'm with ya."

"Good, that's what I want to hear." Henry returned facing forward and let his eyes roam over the surrounding area, finally settling on a group of parked cars off to the right, fifty feet from the crowd. There was plenty of cover to reach these vehicles and Henry worked out a plan in his mind for a diversion that should do the job. Of course, a lot of his plan had to do with luck, but it wouldn't be the first time he'd gambled and won. The day Death called his bluff he'd be ready, but till then he would keep moving forward and never look back.

"Okay, I have a plan."

"I'm all ears," Skeeter said, more agreeable than ever before.

Henry pointed to the cars and quickly explained as Skeeter nodded and spit to the side, then nodded and spit again.

Henry didn't know what would happen when he enabled the plan, so when five of the eight cars exploded like giant Roman candles, to say he was surprised would be an understatement. The shock wave rolled outward, knocking more than half the zombies on their asses, the other half stumbling forward as the blast wave hit them. It had been late afternoon, and as the cars ignited, it seemed like it was early morning, the flash so strong it felt like the morning rays of a rising sun when it kissed the horizon.

A few seconds after the initial blast and the ensuing explosions had passed, Henry and Skeeter jumped up from their hiding place and dashed for the entrance to the hospital, as the undead slowly regained their feet.

Henry's plan was simple. He and Skeeter had crawled over to the group of parked cars and had slid a piece of cloth into each gas tank. Finding the cloth had been easy as there were desiccated corpses lying everywhere and it was simple to tear off a shirt here or a pant leg there.

Henry hadn't thought there would be much gas in the tanks because either scavengers had drained them or from simple evaporation, but he hadn't taken into account the fact that the walking dead had never left the hospital and so the tanks had never been tapped, no one wanting to venture close and take the risk.

The cloth wicks that had stayed lit burned until the vapors caught, and then one at a time the tanks had erupted in a glorious fireball that had gone far beyond the diversion he'd wanted.

Still, he wasn't going to complain when good fortune presented itself.

With his Glock in his right hand and the panga in his left, he and Skeeter ran for the hospital entrance. A few zombies spotted them and Henry made sure to take them down with a swipe of the panga, not wanting so much as one ghoul to follow them. He knew from past experience if even one saw him and followed, more would do the same, as if it was some kind of instinctual thing with the undead.

Skeeter used his sawed-off like a club and took down two zombies that began to stumble towards him. Both went down with crushed skulls, their gray brains leaking out and onto the pavement as their limbs twitched their last.

The two men reached the entrance in seconds of their initial dash, and stopped as they ran inside the hospital. Henry surveyed the shattered glass doors, shaking his head as he did so. "This isn't good, there's no way to block these doors, and if they were open like this, there's bound to be more deaders inside the building."

"No shit," Skeeter said and spit a wad of tobacco juice to the side. "Tell me somethin' I don't now."

"Well, there's nothing we can do about it now. Let's get what we need and go before the diversion wears off."

Skeeter shrugged as he looked at Henry. "Well, shit, don't look at me. I got you here. I don't know my way around the inside of this place anymore than you do."

"Great, I didn't think of that. Okay, let's split up and meet back here in the lobby in fifteen minutes."

"Okay, good luck," Skeeter said and ran off.

"Yeah, you too." Henry ran the other way, searching for signs that would steer him in the right direction.

As the two men ran off, neither bothered to look outside again.

A zombie had spotted Skeeter just as the man had slipped inside the hospital, and it began its slow, plodding walk to the entrance.

A few more spotted this lone zombie who seemed to have a purpose, and in time, they too, joined the first.

By the time the first zombie was halfway to the entrance, more than a dozen had joined it. And worse, the diversion had worked a little too well, for though it had distracted the zombies in the immediate vicinity, it was also like a giant beacon to any within a mile radius. Some were much closer and they began to follow the smoke as it drifted lazily into the sky.

Henry's boots crunched on scattered debris that lined the hall-way he was running down. The dried husks of aged corpses were everywhere, left out like so much old laundry. Flies flittered about, trying to seek nourishment from the corpses. The smell was pungent but had declined with age.

He'd smelled much worse in his time among the walking dead. As he ran, his eyes darted back and forth, peering into the gloom of hospital rooms. He saw brown liquid splattered on many walls and doors—obviously dried blood. He stepped over body parts that were so decayed they looked as if they would blow away in a stiff wind.

Soon, he reached the nurse's station and he leaned over the counter, his panga held high if there were any surprises.

So far the hospital was abandoned by both the living and the dead. Good, he didn't need anything slowing him down, and if there were zombies in the building, they would only be a nuisance.

There was a map on the wall to the right of the nurse's station and he quickly found where he was. After a full thirty seconds of studying it, he found what he was looking for. Racing down a branching hallway, he made his way to where he hoped the drugs would be stored. Behind him, his passing caused papers from old files to blow around and then settle on the floor once more.

Skeeter found the pharmacology closet and kicked in the door, the lock breaking easily. When the building had been operational, only hospital personal were allowed access to this part of the building so there was no need for heavy duty locks.

Entering the room, he found rows of shelving units facing him. The air was slightly fresher inside the room, well, compared to how it was in the hallway with bodies piled up like cordwood along the walls. There had been some serious dying going on here once upon a time.

He reached into his pocket and withdrew a piece of paper. On it was a list made by Doc Connors of all the meds he was in need of. Skeeter squinted slightly, his eyes trying to focus. He'd needed glasses even before the dead walked but had been too stubborn to get a pair. Now, it was too late as eye doctors were few and far between, if there were any still alive at all.

He picked up a basket on the floor and began searching the shelves for the correct medications. As he read the labels, he scratched his head. They all looked the damn same to him, with names so long he could barely pronounce them. Then he found one that the doctor had said was an antibiotic and he smiled widely, proud of himself. He reached an arm up, wrapped them around the bottles, then slid them all off the shelf and into the basket in one wide sweep.

Gloating inwardly, he began searching for more items on the list. He moved to the second aisle and began reading the bottles one at a time. By the twelfth, he spotted another antibiotic. Feeling good and lucky, he reached up to neck height and wrapped both arms around the bottles, not caring if he got a few that weren't on the list mixed in. It was as he did this, his arms spread out on the shelf, that a zombie popped up and sank its teeth into the upper section of his right wrist.

Cursing a scream, he yanked his arms back before the zombie could good get a good bite. Instead of losing a chunk of his flesh, the wound was barely bleeding. But it *was* bleeding. He knew what that meant, though at the moment he didn't want to face it. For now, revenge on the creature that had killed him was the only thing on his mind.

Dropping the basket of pills, he reached for his .45 and placed it an inch before the zombie's face, as it hissed and groaned, its cracked and dry lips covered in Skeeter's blood. Just before he pulled the trigger, the ghoul slid its black tongue out of its mouth and licked its upper lip to savor the blood there.

The bullet struck the face a quarter inch above the nose, then penetrated the brain before blowing out the back of the skull in a spray of bone and brain matter. The white eyes seemed to look inward, as if the zombie was trying to see the entrance hole in its face. Then the head snapped back from the concussion and the body dropped from sight.

Muttering every swear word imaginable, Skeeter went to a shelf piled high with bandages and grabbed three packages, then went to a row with antiseptic spray.

Tearing open one package of bandages with his teeth, he used it to clean the wound, then applied the spray and followed it by wrapping his wrist with another fresh bandage. When he was finished, he pulled his sleeve down on his arm and was pleased to see the white bandage was hidden.

No one would know what happened here and, hey, maybe he would be lucky and would be fine. It could happen; there was no one that had ever said it hadn't. He could be immune, one in a million even.

He went back to the basket, picked it up, and gathered what plastic white bottles had spilled out of it, then walked around to admire his handiwork. The zombie wore hospital scrubs and a white lab coat.

It was hard to tell for sure but Skeeter figured the man had been a doctor, and after becoming infected had either sought shelter in the supply room or had been trapped here after turning. Either way, the bastard had been waiting for him and now Skeeter had a wound and an uncertain future. He kicked the corpse once in the side for good measure, wanting to do more but stopping himself. He'd blown its head off; what more could he do to it?

Checking his wristwatch, he saw he was running out of time before meeting up with Henry, so pushing down his thoughts and his concern for his bite, he got back to work searching for medical supplies.

Eight minutes later, Henry and Skeeter met up in the hallway leading to the lobby, the shattered doors clearly visible from their vantage point. Only that wasn't the only thing visible.

As the two men stood staring, a crowd of zombies began stumbling through the hollow door frames to enter the lobby.

"Shhhiiiitttt," Skeeter spit when he saw the wave of ghouls coming directly for him and Henry.

"No time to worry about it now," Henry said. Over one shoulder, he carried a white sheet, the four corners tied into a knot. Inside it, the contents rattled as the bottles of pills he'd found bounced around. "Back the way we came. We can get out another way." He shot the first ghoul in line, its head exploding in a bloody mess of bone and brains as it collapsed to the floor. The others had to step over or around it but it did little to slow down the encroaching mass.

Skeeter had found a backpack, taken from a desiccated husk he'd found in a room. The pack had been hanging on the door and in the bed was the dried-out body of a long-gone patient. He'd thought the body might have been of a woman, but he may have been wrong. In a hospital gown and nothing else, gender was hard to figure out. He'd transferred the bottles of pills he'd found into the backpack for easy carrying.

The two men retreated deeper into the hospital, searching for another exit. Their feet echoed in the halls and flies flew off the bodies, angered at the disruption in the air as the two men breezed by.

Behind them, the dead shuffled into the lobby, moving off in different directions. Like red dye poured into water, they spread out, swarming through the corridors of the hospital.

Rounding a corner, both men came up short and had to stop running when they saw that the access doors leading out of this section of the hospital were not only chained up, but also were piled high with desks and other assorted furniture, such as office chairs and televisions with broken screens.

"What the fuck!" Skeeter screamed. "What asshole did this?"

"Probably the staff," Henry said. "When everything fell apart, they probably tried to barricade themselves in or to keep the deaders out. Now it's trapped us, too."

"Fuck that," Skeeter hissed. "Give me a hand." He ran at the barricade and began tearing at the furniture. Most were so intertwined he had trouble getting even one chair out of the pile. He cursed some more as he worked, getting nowhere fast. He turned to Henry, his eyes wide with either fear or anger. "Don't just fucking stand there, Henry! Help me!"

Henry was about to do just that when shuffling feet echoed from down the hallway. Turning his head, a second later the first of the undead pursuers appeared. Raising his Glock, Henry shot the zombie in the neck, doing little damage other than a bullet hole. Cursing his bad aim, he raised his gun a few inches and fired again, and this time was rewarded with the ghoul dropping. But more were right behind it.

Skeeter was still tearing at the barricade and didn't see the zombies. Henry stepped over to him, grabbed his arm, and pulled him away from the blocked doors. "Forget it, there's no time! They're here!" he yelled.

Skeeter turned and saw the zombies filling the hallway and screamed in rage. Slinging the sawed-off shotgun off his shoulder, he fired three times, cutting bodies in half, but there were more still coming, and Henry knew no matter how much Skeeter wanted to, he didn't have enough shells to take them all down. Reaching out again, he grabbed Skeeter's arm and dragged the man into an adjoining hallway. "This way, we need to keep moving."

Reluctantly, Skeeter let Henry pull him and the two men began running again. They reached the end of the hallway and another set of double doors, these doors also blocked with furniture.

"There, the fire door!" Henry yelled. The door was chained but Henry shot the padlock off it, then shot the lock on the actual door, followed by kicking it in. It opened onto a small cement landing, only leading upward. "In here, maybe we'll have better luck on the second floor."

Skeeter dashed into the landing, Henry right behind him. Henry slammed the fire door closed but there was no way to lock it from the inside. Leaving it, he ran up the stairs, Skeeter's stomping footsteps just above him.

He burst out onto the second floor a few seconds after Skeeter, and both men looked around the hallway they stood in. Fifteen feet down was the nurse's station, and huddling around it, like nurses taking a break from rounds, were more than a dozen zombies, all wearing hospital scrubs. The staff had been trapped on the second floor for almost two years and needless to say they were very hungry. 'Rounds' were over, it was time to feed.

Like wild animals, they all spun to face the two breathless men, then began moving at a fast walk towards them. Henry turned and was planning on going back the way he'd come, but he heard the moans of the dead as they entered the stairwell.

"We're not going back that way," Henry said and shot two zombies that had once been doctors. Skeeter shot a candystriper, nearly cutting the female zombie in half, then shifted his aim and fired again.

"And we can't keep running around this place. We'll get cornered for sure and when we run out of ammo, that'll be all she wrote."

Henry knew Skeeter was right. One glance down the north hallway and he could see that the doors had been barricaded like on the first floor. He had a flash of what it must have been like when the hospital became inundated with sick and dying people.

There were those that had died and returned, but at the time, no one would have understood what was truly happening, that the sick people weren't simply ill. It would have only been later, when those same sick people had started attacking their living caretakers, that the true horror would have begun. So the staff had barricaded themselves inside the wards of the hospital, hoping to wait it out until help arrived. Only help never arrived and perhaps there had been a zombie already among them, maybe in one of the patient rooms.

There were still unanswered questions of course. Such as how so many zombies had been in one area. Back when the contaminated rain first fell, and before that when to drink the water of the small town was a death sentence, the virus hadn't been contagious by a bite. If a zombie bit someone, they were fine other than having a bad wound that might get infected. Only in time did the virus mutate and become infectious by a bite.

Henry shook his head, deciding all these questions didn't mean a damn thing. All that mattered was escaping the hospital and returning with the meds to save Mary.

"This way!" Henry yelled and took off running towards the barricaded double doors he'd seen moments ago.

"But that way's blocked!" Skeeter called after him.

Before Henry reached the blocked doors, he turned into one of the patients' rooms. Skeeter followed, and upon entering the room, Henry kicked the door closed and pushed the bed in front of it. There was no lock on the door.

"Why the hell did you come in here?" Skeeter asked. "Now we're trapped."

"No, we were trapped out there. In here we have an escape route."

The door shook as the zombies reached it and both Skeeter and Henry pushed their shoulders into the bed, holding back the onslaught of corpses. Unfortunately, the bed was on wheels and they barely managed to keep the door closed. With each passing second, more zombies were pushing on the door, until the entire crowd of undead hospital staff was surging forward.

"What the fuck are you talking about?"

Henry didn't reply to the older man, but turned and shot the large glass window that lined the outer wall of the room. Three placed shots, all a foot from one another in a triangular pattern. The window didn't shatter, as it was safety glass, but it did star slightly.

"You got this?" Henry asked of Skeeter to hold the bed in place.

"Sure, I can hold 'em off for a minute or two."

"Good." Henry jumped away from the bed and picked up a chair in the corner of the room, then swung it hard as he could at the window, aiming for the bullet holes. The first blow caused the window to crack some more but still it didn't break. The chair bounced off the window and almost hit Skeeter. Henry smiled an apology and picked the chair up again, then slammed it at the glass once more. This time the window shattered, shards of glass raining down to the ground two stories below.

The bed shifted and the first zombie fell inside the room, landing heavily. There were more right behind it. Skeeter leveled his shotgun and fired point blank at the crowd in the doorway. The blast sliced the first body in half and peppered the one behind it with so much damage it resembled nothing more than a pile of mush.

He ejected the spent shells and reached into a pocket for some more. He didn't like what he felt, which was only a few more shells.

A zombie crawled under the bed and was about to sink its teeth into Skeeter's ankle when Henry fired his Glock at the jutting head. It was knocked to the floor from the force of the bullet that impacted it directly over the right ear, then took out most of its teeth. Skeeter glanced at Henry and nodded in thanks for the save, Henry giving him a slight nod in return. The two men were warriors battling the living dead, it was a bond some men would never understand until they were thrown into the thick of it. As far as Henry was concerned, Skeeter was blood kin now, the two men relying on one another to survive into the next minute.

"Time to go," Henry said, and without waiting for a reply, he jumped out the window. The wind whistled by his head as the cool air caressed his sweaty body. He saw the sun had gone done and night had fallen. Though the drop took less than three seconds, it felt like an hour and he readied himself for the impact, knowing it could be bad. If he landed wrong, he could break a leg or worse, and if that happened, the odds of him seeing the sun rise were slim to none.

Though he thought he was ready for the landing, it came far too quickly and he felt his feet hit the ground before his body could act. A sharp pain slid up his right foot from the ankle, then soared through his torso and into his brain. He cried out and fell to the ground hard, the wind knocked out of him. He rolled with the fall and absorbed some of the landing, but it was too little too late to prevent an injury.

Lying on his back as he tried to catch his breath, he tried to guess the damage his leg had sustained. Images of him looking down at his ankle and seeing bone protruding through his flesh came to him, and as he sat up and looked, he let out a massive sigh to see he was still whole, his bones inside his body where they belonged.

Reaching down, he touched the tender ankle and cried out again. It was either broken or sprained. Not that it mattered. Getting to his feet, he hobbled on the bad ankle, and though he was as slow as an old man with arthritis, he could still walk. He picked up a fallen tree branch on the ground from a nearby oak tree and used it to help him stay upright.

He saw movement above, and a second later, Skeeter came tumbling out the window. When the man landed, he landed much harder than Henry and he screamed as his left leg snapped in half, the bone jutting out of the skin the way Henry had been terrified had happened to him. With Skeeter screaming in pain, Henry hobbled over to him and knelt down beside him.

"Quiet, man, you'll call every damn deader in the area to us."

"You fucking be quiet! Jesus it hurts! That's what I get from jumping out a fucking window! What was I thinking?"

Henry was inspecting the wound. "You were thinking you were a minute away from getting eaten and decided that following me was a better bet. That's what you were thinking."

A low moan from above caused Henry to look up and what he saw made his blood run cold. The zombies were at the shattered window and they cared nothing for heights. One at a time, they began walking out the window, tumbling ass over elbow through the air. Acting fast, Henry grabbed Skeeter's shirt collar and dragged the man away from under the window. No sooner did

Skeeter get pulled away, than the first ghoul landed heavily. It plopped down head first and its neck snapped like a dry twig. But the others behind it were more fortunate and now had their brethren to land on. Many were unhurt and slowly rose to their feet to continue the pursuit.

"Shit, it's time to go again. I think we wore out our welcome," Henry said as he lifted Skeeter up and began to half-carry the man. It wouldn't have been so bad if Henry didn't have a bad ankle on top of it.

Together, looking like two men on their last legs, they began to hobble away from the hospital, the zombies following right behind.

Skeeter yelled out more than once from the pain and Henry had to shush the man. Skeeter would apologize, only to cry out again. Henry felt the man's pain, especially after seeing the blood and the bone poking out of his pant leg, but he needed Skeeter to remain quiet or they would never escape.

When they reached the parking lot, Henry wanted to let out a sigh of relief, but it quickly changed to mumbled curses when he saw that the parking lot had three times as many zombies as before, thanks to the car explosions. And they were all looking right at the two men, no doubt thanks to Skeeter's cries of agony.

"This way," Henry said and began to hobble them away from the hospital as the dead turned and began to follow.

Before they had gone twenty feet, the undead horde began catching up. More came at the two men from the side, and Henry shot body after body. Skeeter did the same, his jaw tight as he fought off the pain. He expelled all his shotgun shells and let the weapon hang from his shoulder, then drew his .45 and began shooting at anything that moved, only with the pain filling his head, many of his shots missed completely. It wasn't long before his gun clicked on empty.

They became blocked in as more ghouls circled around them, but Henry wasn't about to give up. Shooting two zombies on the far right of the line, he charged the rest like a football player, Skeeter basically dragged along with him. He hit three ghouls in the chest and stomach, knocking them to the ground, then forced his way through and kept going.

Henry had five bullets left if he'd counted right and he used them sparingly.

As he hobbled along, his left arm was wrapped around Skeeter, his right holding the Glock. His ankle was screaming at him, and it felt like molten lead was covering his foot. Still, he trudged on, for Mary, for himself, and for Skeeter.

But it was becoming clear there was no way he and Skeeter were going to make it through this, not together anyway. Henry thought he'd probably be nimble enough to do it alone, but with Skeeter dragging him down, well, there was no way.

But that didn't stop him from trying. He would never leave a man behind, never, and to do so was against everything he was made of.

But then something occurred that changed everything, something he would never have known if not for a few actions happening simultaneously.

The first was Skeeter tripped and fell to the ground. The second was the sleeve on his right arm rode up, exposing his wrist. The third was the moon peeked out from behind its cloud cover and illuminated the area, and the fourth was Henry saw the fresh bandage on Skeeter's arm, and he'd known it wasn't there before they'd entered the hospital.

Henry reached down and tore off the bandage. Fearing the worst, he got what he expected. There, in a shallow impression in Skeeter's skin, were the unmistakable indents of teeth marks...human teeth marks. Small droplets of blood beaded around the wound and on the inside of the bandage.

"You were bit. Why didn't you say something?" Henry asked as he hauled the man to his feet and they began shuffling away. Henry shot two more zombies that got within a few feet of him and Skeeter.

"What's there to say?"

"So you planned on keeping it to yourself? You know what a bite means."

"So fucking what? Maybe I'll be fine, you don't know I'll turn," Skeeter said through tight breaths. "Ah, Jesus, ease up will ya, it fucking hurts!"

Henry didn't say anything in reply; he was thinking heavily on a difficult subject. He was weighing his options and his moral code.

Ten second ago, before he'd seen Skeeter had been bitten, he would have done anything to save the man, and either they both would have escaped or neither of them would.

But things had suddenly changed dramatically, and Henry knew that in the world he now lived in, sometimes the only law was the one of survival. He needed to slow the zombies down so he could make a break for it and reach his motorcycle, but there was only one thing that would cause the ghouls to stop chasing him.

They needed something else to feed on.

He stopped moving and let go of Skeeter, the man balancing precariously on one leg. "Hey, what the fuck!" he snapped, not understanding what was happening.

"I'm sorry, there's no other option," Henry said coldly and pulled his panga from its sheath and slid it across Skeeter's abdomen. The blade was as sharp as ever and it sliced into Skeeter like the man was made of warm butter. As his gut spilled open, his intestines poured out to splash onto the ground and the man's feet.

Skeeter was speechless as he stared down at his insides spilling out of him like too many worms in a bait sack. He went to his knees, his broken leg no longer an issue as his insides met the chill air, giving off what looked like steam.

Henry reached over and sliced the backpack off Skeeter's shoulder, knowing the meds had to come with him, then he turned and began hobbling away, making much better time and moving twice as fast as the zombies. He used up the last of his bullets on a pair of ghouls trying to flank him, then his Glock clicked on empty and he holstered it and relied on his panga if any got too close.

Skeeter looked up from his exposed insides to see Henry moving away. Skeeter's face was a mask of betrayal, as he stared at the retreating man. "How could you do this to me? You're murdering me! You bastard! Come back here!"

"I'm sorry, Skeeter! You were dead anyway!" Henry yelled over his shoulder as he kept his running-hobble up. "You were gonna die from that bite! I'm sorry, I truly am! It has to be this way. One of us needs to make it out of here alive!"

"You son-of-a-bitch! I'll see you in Hell! I'll see you in fucking Hell! I'll be waiting for you, you fucker! I'll be waiting for you!"

Then the zombies were on him, tearing at his body, pulling at his intestines, biting into his exposed face and neck. Skeeter began to scream, and soon he started to shriek, as he was torn apart limb by limb, gutted and fed on while still alive.

As Henry made his way down the road, he kept waiting for Skeeter to stop cursing him, to stop screaming, but it seemed to continue for far longer than Henry would ever have imagined.

Finally, Skeeter's throat was torn out and the screams turned to gargles, then silence, only the sounds of the feeding frenzy filling the night.

Henry never turned around to see if he was being followed closely, for it didn't matter whether the zombies were following him or not. All he could do was keep moving and hope he made it to the motorcycle before he was caught.

Eventually, he reached the two parked motorcycles and he climbed onto the one that was his. As he looked down the road behind him, he saw nothing. No ghouls had followed him, all of them content to feed on Skeeter.

Starting the engine, he gritted his teeth as he placed his bad foot onto the foot peg. His ankle was on fire, the pain so powerful it was like a living entity. Setting his jaw, he positioned the backpack taken from Skeeter over his shoulders and set the sheet-wrapped bottles on the gas tank between his legs, then drove off.

Though guilt filled him for what he'd done to survive, he knew it would all be worth it if it saved Mary's life. Sometimes, survival was all that mattered; the rest was just the bullshit men made up to justify their actions.

This wasn't the first time he'd done something he knew would haunt him in his dreams, and if he continued to fight and survive, he knew it wouldn't be the last.

There were always hard choices to make, and anyone who didn't want to make them, would join the dead sooner or later.

One week later, Mary was sitting up in bed and feeling like her old self. Her wound was healing nicely and Henry planned on leaving with her and the others the next morning if she was up for it.

She was and couldn't wait to get out of the doctor's home, feeling cabin fever like never before. His ankle was still sore but healing quickly also. Other than a slight limp, he could get around fine.

Doc Connors was more than happy with the meds Henry had brought back and they more than covered the cost of taking care of Mary, as well as for food and board for the companions for the length of their stay.

There was even enough payment leftover for the group to re-arm themselves with enough ammunition to get them to wherever they were going next, plus some dried food.

For once, no one got into any trouble in the local taverns. Cindy told Henry there had been a few close calls but she had managed to keep Jimmy out of trouble.

After meeting with the General, and Henry had explained they were leaving, he'd half expected the man to try and stop him, but the General had merely shook his hand and wished him well.

It was a nice change from all the times it seemed the men in charge would try to use Henry and his people to further their own malevolent ends.

When Doc Connors asked what had become of Skeeter, Henry had simply explained that the man had been attacked and killed by zombies when caught off guard.

There was no reason to go into it any further. What was done was done and Henry would take the secret of what he'd done to the man to his grave.

He remembered Skeeter's last words to him, telling Henry he would see him in Hell. Henry couldn't help but find that a little ironic. After all the evil men he'd sent on the last train west, he had a feeling Skeeter was going to have to get in line when it came to people in Hell waiting for Henry to arrive.

But till then, he was alive, and he would cherish each day for what it was...a gift.

The next morning, the companions walked out of the compound by using the same ramp they'd entered with. The zombies that had chased them there were all gone.

Most had been put down, the bodies burned, but others had simply wandered away after seeing something that caught their attention.

There was no choice where to go first. Henry wanted their car back and if he was lucky, it would still be sitting in front of his house, exactly where they'd left it.

The guards on the fence waved as the group of six exited the compound and began their slow trek back to Henry's neighborhood.

Mary wasn't up to her peak yet but was getting better with each passing hour. The fresh air was doing her loads of good.

Jimmy and Cindy walked point together, Henry and Mary were in the middle, and Sue and Raven walked side by side in the rear, talking together.

Mary leaned over and kissed Henry on the cheek as they walked and he looked surprised by it. "What was that for?" he asked as he touched his cheek with a callused hand.

"I just wanted to thank you again. I can't imagine what it was like out there for you, all alone after Skeeter died. And you did it all for me."

He reached out and touched her cheek. "I'd do it again for you if I had to. I told you before that I'd never let anything bad happen to you and I meant it. I'll keep you safe with everything I have."

"Oh really? Nice sentiment, but if it's true, then how do you explain this?" She pointed to her bad leg. She was limping slightly but her leg felt better the more she walked.

"Hey, now, just wait one second there. I didn't say I was God. I can't be everywhere at once, and I never said you being clumsy was part of the deal."

She laughed and her face lit up and Henry felt good, knowing it hadn't all been for nothing.

"Hey, what are you two talking about up there?" Sue called.

Mary turned slightly. "Oh nothing, just thanking your man for being so brave."

Sue sped up and wrapped her arms around Henry's waist. "He is brave, isn't he? My big strong guy."

Henry began to blush. "Will you two quit it, please?"

"What's the matter, old man? Can't you take it?" Jimmy called back, chuckling. Then he said in a women's voice, *"Oh, Henry, you're so brave. Oh, Henry, thank you for saving me. I loooove you, Henry.*" He made kissing sounds as he walked backwards. Then, "Hey, ow, why'd you do that?" he asked Cindy, who had smacked him on the back of the head.

"'Cause you're being a jerk. Cut it out."

"Or what?"

"Or no sex for a week," Cindy warned.

That got Jimmy's attention. "Okay, okay, I'm sorry. I won't do it anymore." Cindy turned around and continued walking and Jimmy blew Henry one last kiss and smirked, before spinning around. He slapped Cindy on the butt and she squealed and punched him in the arm—hard. He muttered a curse and kept walking.

Behind the two lovers, the others laughed and Raven ran up and jumped on Jimmy's back, the two playing a little.

Henry wrapped his right arm around Sue's shoulder and his left around Mary's waist and smiled as he walked. In the world of the living dead, there were hard choices to make, and anyone who didn't want to make them would join the dead sooner or later.

Hell yes, it had been worth it.

Epilogue

After finding the car untouched, they found their lost backpacks, still where they'd dropped them, and climbed into the car and drove off, leaving the smoking ruin that was Henry's house. Evidently, the fire had burned itself out and the entire neighborhood hadn't been consumed.

Sue, Raven and Cindy didn't recognize the route Henry took, but Jimmy and Mary most definitely did.

As Henry swung off the main road, they passed a telephone repair truck, the cherry picker canted at an odd angle from so many years of being held aloft.

There was a zombie on the back of the truck, impaled on the tools, but it didn't look like it was still functioning. After years of remaining impaled there, it had slowly rotted away into nothing.

The car sped fast down the dirt road, blowing dust on the zombie. Whether it moved on its own or it was just the wind would never be known.

The car drove up the road and Jimmy and Mary looked out the car windows with haunted eyes. They were going back to where it all began; back to Pineridge Laboratories.

Henry parked before the shattered main doors, remembering the last time he'd been here. It was after they'd buried Scott and Blackie.

As Henry turned off the engine and opened his door, he shifted in his seat to look at Sue, Raven and Cindy one at a time, then said, "If it's okay with you guys, I'd like to just be with Jimmy and Mary for a bit. Then we'll call you over."

Sue nodded. "Sure, Henry, I understand."

Raven shrugged, not really caring either way, and Cindy said she was okay with it. She leaned over and kissed Jimmy once, consoling him. She could see the past swirling in his eyes, then she took his hand and squeezed it, nodding that she was fine with her staying in the car.

Jimmy and Mary climbed out and joined Henry.

"Are we going inside?" Jimmy asked, his voice almost a whisper.

Henry shrugged. "I wasn't planning on it. There's nothing in there we need. You can if you want to though."

"No, I'm fine," he said and Mary nodded in agreement.

The three friends walked to the side of the building and to the two graves located under a copse of trees. Off to the right were the remnants of a funeral pyre, a few tell-tale skulls visible in the soot that had hardened to a charcoal-like consistency after so many years.

They stood side by side, just like they had done two years ago, and looked down at the two graves. Mary knelt down and cleared some weeds from them, as Jimmy and Henry looked on.

"Should we say anything?" Jimmy asked, his eyes clouded with emotion. He was thinking about Scott Peterson, how the two had become fast friends, and how in one moment of dropping his guard, Scott had been attacked and killed by zombies.

Jimmy had gone over that day a million times in his head, regretting his actions leading up to the attack, for if he hadn't been so cocky, it was possible Scott wouldn't have died that day.

Mary was on her knees, staring at Blackie's grave. The Black Lab had become one of the team, and had died protecting Henry, her and Jimmy. She missed him a lot and wished things had been different.

"No, Jimmy, I think we've said all that needs to be said," Henry added as he gazed down at the graves. So many memories, so many things he might have done differently if he'd known what he did now back then.

But regrets were something he had in bucketfuls and had learned to live with.

Mary wiped the tears from her eyes as she stood up, then went to Henry, who hugged her.

She glanced back to the front of the building to see Raven, Sue and Cindy standing quietly, giving the trio their space but watching and wanting to take part in whatever ritual they were enacting.

"Can I call them over now?" Mary asked.

Henry followed her gaze and saw Sue and the others. "Sure, let's have our entire family here now." He waved for the others to join them and everyone sat down by the graves as Henry began to talk.

"I don't think any of us have ever told you what happened here at Pineridge. How we all met up and became a family."

Cindy looked at Jimmy and said to Henry. "Never heard it all. I've asked a few times but Jimmy will never tell me the whole thing."

"Well, it's time you heard it," Henry said. Sue was sitting next to him and he pulled her close. She leaned to the side and placed her head on his shoulder, then he reached out and took Mary's hand, squeezing it softly.

To Jimmy he just nodded, the younger man doing the same. Henry gestured to the graves. "The two that are buried here were once part of our family. Blackie was a black Labrador we adopted when we found him and, well, I guess so was Scott Peterson." He leaned back and sighed as he let the memories of the past wash over him. "Here's how it all began…"

DEAD WORLDS: Undead Stories
A Zombie Anthology Volume 1
Edited by Anthony Giangregorio

Welcome to the world of the dead, where the laws of nature have been twisted, reality changed.

The Dead Walk!

Filled with established and promising new authors for the next generation of corpses, this anthology will leave you gasping for air as you go from one terror-filled story to another.

Like the decomposing meat of a freshly rotting carcass, this book will leave you breathless.

Don't say we didn't warn you.

DEAD MOURNING: A ZOMBIE HORROR STORY
by Anthony Giangregorio

Carl Jenkins was having a run of bad luck. Fresh out of jail, his probation tenuous, he'd lost every job he'd taken since being released. So now was his last chance, only one more job to prevent him from going back to prison. Assigned to work in a funeral home, he accidentally loses a shipment of embalming fluid. With nothing to lose, he substitutes it with a batch of chemicals from a nearby factory.

The results don't go as planned, though. While his screw-up goes unnoticed, his machinations revive the cadavers in the funeral home, unleashing an evil on the world that it has not seen before. Not wanting to become a snack for the rampaging dead, he flees the city, joining up with other survivors. An old, dilapidated zoo becomes their haven, while the dead wait outside the walls, hungry and patient.

But Carl is optimistic, after all, he's still alive, right? Perhaps his luck has changed and help will arrive to save them all?

Unfortunately, unknown to him and the other survivors, a serial killer has fallen into their group, trapped inside the zoo with them.

With the undead army clamoring outside the walls and a murderer within, it'll be a miracle if any of them live to see the next sunrise.

On second thought, maybe Carl would've been better off if he'd just gone back to jail.

VISIONS OF THE DEAD: A ZOMBIE STORY
by Anthony & Joseph Giangregorio

Jake Roberts felt like he was the luckiest man alive.

He had a great family, a beautiful girlfriend, who was soon to be his wife, and a job, that might not have been the best, but it paid the bills.

At least until the dead began to walk. Now Jake is fighting to survive in a dead world while searching for his lost love, Melissa, knowing she's out there somewhere. But the past isn't dead, and as he struggles for an uncertain future, the past threatens to consume him. With the present a constant battle between the living and the dead, Jake finds himself slipping in and out of the past, the visions of how it all happened haunting him. But Jake knows Melissa is out there somewhere and he'll find her or die trying. In a world of the living dead, you can never escape your past.

DEAD WORLDS: Undead Stories
A Zombie Anthology Volume 2
Edited by Anthony Giangregorio

Welcome to a world where the dead walk and want nothing more than to feast on the living. The stories contained in this, the second volume of the Dead Worlds series, are filled with action, gore, and buckets and buckets of blood; plus a heaping side of entrails for those with a little extra hunger.

The stories contained within this volume are scribed by both the desiccated cadavers of seasoned veterans to the genre as well as fresh-faced corpses, each printed here for the first time; and all of them ready to dig in and please the most discerning reader.

So slap on a bib and prepare to get bloody, because you're about to read the best zombie stories this side of Hell!

ROAD KILL: A ZOMBIE TALE
by Anthony Giangregorio

ORDER UP! In the summer of 2008, a rogue comet entered earth's orbit for 72 hours. During this time, a strange amber glow suffused the sky. But something else happened; something in the comet's tail had an adverse affect on dead tissue and the result was the reanimation of every dead animal carcass on the planet. A handful of survivors hole up in a diner in the backwoods of New Hampshire while the undead creatures of the night hunt for human prey. There's a new blue plate special at DJ's Diner and Truck Stop, and it's you!

THE DARK

by Anthony Giangregorio

The darkness came without warning.

First New York, then the rest of United States, and then the world became enveloped in a perpetual night without end.

With no sunlight, eventually the planet will wither and die, bringing on a new Ice Age. But that isn't problem for the human race, for humanity will be dead long before that happens.

There is something in the dark, creatures only seen in nightmares, and they are on the prowl. Evolution has changed and man is no longer the dominant species. When we are children, we're told not to fear the dark, that what we believe to exist in the shadows is false.

Unfortunately, that is no longer true.

SOULEATER

by Anthony Giangregorio

Twenty years ago, Jason Lawson witnessed the brutal death of his father by something only seen in nightmares, something so horrible he'd blocked it from his mind. Now twenty years later the creature is back, this time for his son. Jason won't let that happen.

He'll travel to the demon's world, struggling every second to rescue his son from its clutches. But what he doesn't know is that the portal will only be open for a finite time and if he doesn't return with his son before it closes, then he'll be trapped in the demon's dimension forever.

SEE HOW IT ALL BEGAN IN THE NEW DOUBLE-SIZED 460 PAGE SPECIAL EDITION!
DEADWATER: EXPANDED EDITION

by Anthony Giangregorio

Through a series of tragic mishaps, a small town's water supply is contaminated with a deadly bacterium that transforms the town's population into flesh eating ghouls. Without warning, Henry Watson finds himself thrown into a living hell where the living dead walk and want nothing more than to feed on the living.

Now Henry's trying to escape the undead town before he becomes the next victim. With the military on one side, shooting civilians on sight, and a horde of bloodthirsty zombies on the other, Henry must try to battle his way to freedom. With a small group of survivors, including a beautiful secretary and a wise-cracking janitor to aid him, the ragtag group will do their best to stay alive and escape the city codenamed: **Deadwater**.

DEAD END: A ZOMBIE NOVEL

by Anthony Giangregorio

THE DEAD WALK! Newspapers everywhere proclaim the dead have returned to feast on the living! A small group of survivors hole up in a cellar, afraid to brave the masses of animated corpses, but when food runs out, they have no choice but to venture out into a world gone mad.

What they will discover, however, is that the fall of civilization has brought out the worst in their fellow man. Cannibals, psychotic preachers and rapists are just some of the atrocities they must face. In a world turned upside down, it is life that has hit a Dead End.

DEAD RAGE

by Anthony Giangregorio

An unknown virus spreads across the globe, turning ordinary people into bloodthirsty, ravenous killers. Only a small percentage of the population is immune and soon become prey to the infected.

Amongst the infected comes a man, stricken by the virus, yet still retaining his grasp on reality. His need to destroy the *normals* becomes an obsession and he raises an army of killers to seek out and kill all who aren't *changed* like himself. A few survivors gather together on the outskirts of Chicago and find themselves running for their lives as the specter of death looms over all. The Dead Rage virus will find you, no matter where you hide.

FAMILY OF THE DEAD
A Zombie Anthology

by Anthony, Joseph and Domenic Giangregorio

Clawing their way out of the wet, dark earth, these tales of terror will fill you with the deep seated fear we all have of death and what comes next.

But if that wasn't bad enough to chill your soul, these undead tales are penned by an entire family of corpses. The zombie master himself, Anthony Giangregorio, leads his two young ghouls, his sons Domenic and Joseph Giangregorio, on a journey of terror inducing stories that will keep you up long into the night.

As you read these works of the undead, don't be alarmed by that bump outside the window.

After all, it's probably just a stray tree branch…or is it?

END OF DAYS: AN APOCALYPTIC ANTHOLOGY
VOLUMES 1 AND 2

Our world is a fragile place.

Meteors, famine, floods, nuclear war, solar flares, and hundreds of other calamities can plunge our small blue planet into turmoil in an instant.

What would you do if tomorrow the sun went super nova or the world was swallowed by water, submerging the world into the cold darkness of the ocean? This anthology explores some of those scenarios and plunges you into total annihilation. But remember, it's only a book, and tomorrow will come as it always does. Or will it?

DEADFALL
by Anthony Giangregorio

It's Halloween in the small suburban town of Wakefield, Mass.

While parents take their children trick or treating and others throw costume parties, a swarm of meteorites enter the earth's atmosphere and crash to earth.

Inside are small parasitic worms, no larger than maggots.

The worms quickly infect the corpses at a local cemetery and so begins the rise of the undead.

The walking dead soon get the upper hand, with no one believing the truth. That the dead now walk.

Will a small group of survivors live through the zombie apocalypse?

Or will they, too, succumb to the Deadfall.

DEAD HOUSE: A ZOMBIE GHOST STORY
by Keith Adam Luethke

The old mansion on the edge of town, aptly named Dead House, has a history of blood, pain, and death, but what Victor Leeds knows of this past only scratches the surface of the true horrors within.

But when his girlfriend is attacked by a shadowy figure one rainy night, he soon finds himself caught up in a world where the dead walk and ghostly wraiths abound. And to make matters worse, a pair of serial killers are fulfilling carefully made plans, and when they are done, the small town of Stormville, New York will run red. The last ingredient to open the gates of Hell, and plunge this small upstate town into madness, is rain. And in Stormville, it pours by the gallons.

BOOK OF THE DEAD

Edited by Anthony Giangregorio

This is the most faithful, truest zombie anthology ever written, and we invite you along for the ride. Every single story in this book is filled with slack-jawed, eyes glazed, slow moving, shambling zombies set in a world where the dead have risen and only want to eat the flesh of the living. In these pages, the rules are sacrosanct. There is no deviation from what a zombie should be or how they came about.

The Dead Walk. There is no reason, though rumors and suppositions fill the radio and television stations. But the only thing that is fact is that the walking dead are here and they will not go away. So prepare yourself for the ultimate homage to the master of zombie legend.

And remember... Aim for the head!

DEAD GRAVE (BOOK 8.5)

THE DEADWATER SERIES

by Anthony Giangregorio

Trapped in the mountains of Colorado, Henry Watson and his fellow warrior survivalists find an abandoned cabin and are soon snowed in when a brutal snowstorm arrives. As days turn to weeks, and supplies dwindling, starvation is not out of the question.

Desperate to live one more day, they set out into the arctic weather, praying to find salvation before succumbing to frostbite.

Even in this bleak landscape, the walking dead survive, always searching for their next kill, keeping the companions on their toes.

In their bleakest hour, the group comes upon a mansion hidden in the woods, miles from any form of civilization.

Secluded and off the beaten track, the walking dead are few and far between.

But there are worse things in this new world than the living dead, and if Henry and friends are not careful, they may just find out what that is.

In a world where the dead rule, every man is his own master.

CLAN OF THE BIGFOOT

ANTHONY GIANGREGORIO